HER DESERT PRINCE

MARIE TUHART

Editor: Elizabeth Jewell

Cover Art by Designed by Diana

Formatted by Monica Corwin

Catherine Taylor stretched her sore muscles and blew out a breath. It was a long flight from London to the tiny Middle Eastern country of Bashir, and a smooth one at that. But she hated flying; well, not flying itself, just takeoffs and landings. Now, all she had to do was collect her luggage and drag herself to a taxi.

On her way to baggage claim, she noticed the art on the walls, her artist eyes intrigued by the images of the desert and animals painted there. One wall showed dune after dune of desert sand and the sun sparkling against them. The next wall had a den of sand foxes, cacti, and flowers. She couldn't wait to start her mural at the local hospital for the new children's wing.

While she waited for her luggage, she powered up her cell phone. There were two text messages waiting for her.

One from her manager, letting her know a car had been sent for her, and another from her best friend, Sara.

Catherine texted Sara back, letting her know she'd arrived and she'd call her later. She slid her phone back into her carry-on bag. Within minutes, she had her battered, bright blue suitcase in hand and followed the signs to customs. Thanks to the employment letter from the ruler of Bashir, customs would be a piece of cake.

Exiting the customs door, she glanced around at the people waiting. She didn't see anyone holding a sign with her name. Maybe they were late or waiting outside at pickup.

Halfway to the arrival area, the noise of a large group of men shouting questions at a man walking in her direction caused her to pause. Her attention centered primarily on the man.

His raven hair was disheveled as if some woman had run her fingers through it, and his broad shoulders were straight, adding to his height and his features. His dark brown skin made her think he was of Middle Eastern descent. The man was beyond handsome, an artist's vision, and her fingers itched to pull out her pad and begin sketching. If only she could see his downcast eyes.

The men around him shouted questions in English. Subtle lines appeared around his mouth, and his lips slightly tightened. Something wasn't right. Then he glanced up at her.

Catherine couldn't explain it, but the impact of his

stare caused her to lose her breath. Fire flared to life in his dark eyes. His entire concentration was on her now. A shiver of desire ran through her body at the combination of his dark eyes, strong chin, high cheekbones, and full lips.

Someone jostled her, breaking the contact. With a shake of her head, she breathed and tried to focus her attention away from the man.

It was only then she took note of the people around him. Most of them were reporters with cameras and recording devices. Inside, she cringed and took a deep breath, deciding she needed to avoid that group as much as possible. The pain from Jamie's death didn't hurt as much as before, but she still blamed the paparazzi for hounding her after his death.

Gnawing her lip, she walked on, scanning for a way around the group. But as she moved closer, she couldn't resist looking at the man once more.

He was watching her. Her stomach fluttered along with her pulse as their gazes connected. To her astonishment, he pushed through the crowd and strode straight to her. Her heart pounded. Who was this hot-looking guy? And why was he so interested in her?

"Darling." His husky voice sent shivers up and down her spine. He closed his very masculine hands over her shoulders, stopping her forward progress.

"Excuse me?" Flashes went off, and she barely prevented herself from flinching.

"I'm sorry I'm so late." He tugged her into his embrace. "Please," he whispered, "play along. I'm begging you."

His breath brushed her ear and every nerve in her body went on alert. Jamie had begged her too, and she'd paid dearly for giving in. Her heart pounded. "Who are you?" she whispered. Her mind whirled with the sudden turn of events. Was she going to give into this man? This stranger?

"Later. Trust me, please." He pulled back and framed her face with his palms.

Heat singed her skin, from her cheeks all the way to her toes. Catherine forgot about everyone else except this man. Her feminine side roared to life. Here was a dominant male asking for her help. His straight raven hair begged for her touch, his equally dark eyes gleamed with mischief and desire. And darn if he didn't smell of fresh air and desert.

"I've missed you," he said.

Her jaw almost dropped open at his blatant sensual tone, then she remembered this was all an act. What did he want? More camera flashes went off, and she fought the urge to run away. No, she wasn't a coward anymore, at least she wanted to believe that. He didn't seem to know who she was. Was that a good thing? Yes, she decided it was. The less she was recognized, the better she would feel playing this game.

Her stomach fluttered as she made the decision to help him. The man tapped an index finger against her cheek, and she realized he was waiting for her to play her part in this little vignette.

"I've missed you, too." Releasing her suitcase handle, she slipped her arms around his neck. It was a game she was familiar with; how many times had she and Jamie played it with the paparazzi? Not that Jamie was anything like this man.

An air of danger hung around him, and her body thrummed in response to that danger. "It's been way too long," she murmured, dropping her voice to a whisper.

Hunger flashed in his eyes, and Catherine wondered what the heck she was doing. But then heat from his body—shimmering, smoldering—hit her full force, threatening to blaze her into oblivion. Oh, God, she barely stopped herself from sinking her body against his.

"Way too long," he whispered before he lowered his lips to hers.

The second his mouth touched hers, Catherine realized it was a mistake. His lips were firm, strong, and too tasty. Mint and coffee teased her taste buds. His tongue ran over her lips. She didn't even think, her lips parted instantly for him. He smiled against her mouth before his tongue delved in.

She stiffened, then relaxed as she reminded herself this was all for show. But her body had missed the memo. Her core tingled and heat filled her veins. She hadn't been this romantically close to a man in more than two years. Catherine melted against him and kissed him back.

His hands moved from her cheeks; one grasped the back of her neck, and the other curved around her waist and drew her closer. Yes, her body cried out. Their tongues continued their intricate dance. Electric pulses shot between her core and her breasts, and her nipples tightened.

A flash brought her back to earth with a jolt. Catherine pulled back, but only as far as his arms would let her. His dark eyes were fixed on her face. Up close, she found his eyes weren't as dark as they'd first appeared. They were actually a deep, deep rich brown with gold in them. The gold was molten now, glittering with emotion and lust.

"Umm … " She didn't have a clue what to say. What could she say? She'd never kissed a stranger like that; hell, she hadn't even kissed Jamie with that much passion. And it didn't help that this glorious, sensual man kept staring at her with a hint of a grin, as if to say he wanted to kiss her again.

He started to lower his head, then froze as another camera flash went off. A frown marred his features for a moment before he smiled. "Let's go."

Before she could utter a single word, he grabbed her luggage, and with his arm around her waist, guided her down the concourse. The reporters trailed behind them, and the click of their shutters sounded like crickets in her ears. She wanted to ask him who he was, but he was moving at a fast pace.

The second they stepped outside, a rush of hot air hit her, disorienting her. She didn't have time to process her environment as the man was already pulling her toward an expensive sedan parked near the taxi stand.

The driver snapped up from his lounging position

against the vehicle. "Sir?" He frowned at the reporters behind them. "May I be of service?"

"Yes." The stranger handed the driver her luggage and led her over to the open door before he gestured for her to get in.

She hesitated. "But I don't know you."

"Please," he whispered. "I promise you will be safe."

Maybe it was the honesty shining in his eyes, but Catherine slipped into the cool interior as the driver took his seat. The stranger leaned inside the car, away from the people following them.

"Take the lady wherever she wishes to go, Samir," he said to the driver before turning his gaze to her. "Thank you for saving me."

"But I didn't do much," she said.

"You did enough." He brushed his thumb over her cheek. "Thank you for understanding, darling. I shouldn't be more than an hour." The last was said loud enough for the reporters behind him to hear. Then he straightened and shut the door.

Catherine turned to look out the rear window as the vehicle slid away from the curb. The reporters scrambled to get to their own vehicles, and her stranger was gone.

Still feeling off balance, she rested her fingers on her lips. Did they look as swollen as they felt? His taste lingered, along with the pressure of his mouth against hers. A shiver swept up her spine.

She wanted to taste him again. Sighing, she glanced at

the road behind them, and realized the reporters were following her. That was what she'd wanted to avoid, and here she was thrown right into the middle of it. Well, not quite thrown. When he'd kissed her, she'd gone along with it.

Why? What had she been thinking? She hadn't, and that was the problem. When would she learn not to be tempted by a magnetic man? Catherine gave a small sigh of regret. She'd never see the stranger again; she had no idea of who he was, and he didn't even have her name. No, it was better this way.

"Where are you going, ma'am?" the driver asked.

Gathering her scattered thoughts, she said, "Please take me to the royal palace."

"The palace?"

"Yes. Trust me, I'm expected." She was sure he'd heard it all before, but in her case, it was true.

"Of course, ma'am." The driver smiled and then said quietly, "This is quite unexpected indeed."

Malik al-Hakim strode down the concourse, his mind on the woman he'd placed into his personal vehicle. He regretted putting the paparazzi on her tail, but he didn't have a choice. Too much depended on his being able to meet with the prime minister of Shara in private, and she was the perfect decoy.

Guilt tugged at him, causing his gut to clench. He'd promised himself years ago he'd never let another woman close enough for the press to go after her. Not after such disastrous results the last time. But he had to admit, the woman had been a good sport to play along with him as she had. He was impressed by her performance.

And he hadn't minded kissing her at all. Nor had he minded the softness of her lips, the way her mouth had parted to allow him to taste her, and the way her arms had wound around his neck as if they belonged there.

He'd ask Samir later where he'd taken her. The least Malik could do was to send her flowers with a thank-you card, and he'd include a pass to one of the local spas to make up for all the trouble the press was sure to cause. Hopefully, their interest wouldn't last long. He expected she was a tourist visiting his country, and within a day or two the paparazzi would get tired, especially when he didn't show up to see her.

While he waited for the security doors to open, his mind went back to the embrace he'd shared with her. He'd expected a light, fun kiss, and that's how it had started, but it had quickly turned into something more. Even now he felt her soft lips against his and remembered the slight taste of chocolate from her mouth.

Her pale blue eyes reminded him of the morning sky as he rode through the desert with the sun crested on the horizon. His cock twitched, wondering if her eyes would darken in the throes of passion.

The metal doors swishing open brought Malik out of his musings. Pushing all thoughts about the woman he'd briefly held in his arms out of his mind, he walked into the room.

"Prime minister," Malik greeted, executing a deep bow in respect. Shara was a neighboring country and a country Malik wanted to keep as an ally. The prime minister's dark hair was uncovered. He wore a traditional robe but no hair covering. This was good, as it indicated the prime minister wasn't a traditionalist as Malik had been led to believe. He smiled at Malik, his green eyes gleaming with interest and curiosity.

"Prince Malik, I'm so pleased we could meet privately. Come sit down and we will discuss the issue at hand."

2

Catherine struggled to concentrate on the spectacular sights of the city on the way to the palace, but her mind kept wandering back to the man at the airport. What was it about him that fascinated her? His great bone structure? She shook her head. That was the artist in her, but her emotions told her it was something else.

Oh, hell, her body was still tingling from his embrace. She remembered again his lips firm against hers, his hold strong, and the heat from his body calling to her. Her core tightened.

His mouth had been soft, teasing, and yet questing for more. And she'd kissed him back. But that was a public display, staged for the paparazzi. What would it be like in private, with no one watching? The honking of a horn brought her out of her musings in time to see two men on a moped keeping pace next to the car, one trying to take her picture.

Instinctively, she shrank back, making herself as small as she could. She didn't need this. The paparazzi were not among her favorite people; to say she despised them was putting it mildly. Even with all her exposure as an artist, she kept away from most of the reporters. Her manager was constantly after her to suck up to the press, but she refused. She'd had enough of the press when she was growing up and with Jamie.

Her heart skipped a beat. How Jamie would have loved to have been here with her. He'd found inspiration for his music from the simplest things, and here in Bashir, a city rich with history, Jamie would have had a ball.

She could picture him in one of the open-air plazas with his guitar, a wide smile on his face, alight with happiness while he sang.

A camera flash startled her, and she fought against cringing. If she exposed too much of her fear, they'd exploit it. She was stronger than this, wasn't she? All she could think of was the times Jamie and she were out and the press constantly harassed them, shouting out questions and taking pictures.

"Can you lose them?" she asked the driver. It wouldn't be fair to bring the paparazzi to the king and queen's front door, regardless of whether or not they were used to it. Anger flowed through her, all directed at the stranger at the airport. Why did he send the press after her? He couldn't have dealt with them without involving her? But then she remembered his pleading voice and his eyes as he whispered *please*, and her body tingled with awareness like it never had before.

She sighed. At this rate, she'd never get him out of her head.

"It may be a bit tricky, ma'am, but I'll get rid of them before we get to the palace."

"Thank you." Catherine leaned her head back and closed her eyes, and the driver executed several quick turns.

She caught a few snatches of phrases in Arabic. Probably checking in with his dispatcher. Then she heard sirens.

Opening her eyes, she saw several police vehicles maneuver around them. "What's going on?"

"The authorities will take care of the paparazzi. They know the rules about following anyone." He gave her a smile in the rearview mirror, his brown eyes twinkling. "Now, we can proceed unhampered to the palace."

Catherine let out a breath as she realized the Arabic she'd heard was the driver calling the authorities. His quick thinking eased the knot in her stomach.

The taxi turned, leaving behind the police and the paparazzi. After several more turns, her breath caught in her throat at the sight in front of her.

The palace, looking like something straight out of the *Arabian Nights*, loomed in the background. A large golden gate stood closed, as if protecting the palace and its inhabitants from the world. And in a way, it did. Her fingers itched to sketch the scene before her, but she'd have time later.

The driver pulled up and rolled down his window. A guard in a deep red and gold uniform stepped out of a small guard station. A quick conversation took place in Arabic. Catherine regretted she hadn't had more time to learn the language before she left home. But she caught the words "guest" and "woman" before the gate opened.

Surprise gripped her. She had expected to at least identify herself, but it seemed as if the guards knew her driver. Then she remembered the man at the airport called him by name.

Was that unusual? Probably not. Bashir was a small country, and its capital wasn't huge, so it might not be uncommon to know a taxi driver by name. She shrugged off her thoughts as the vehicle moved forward.

Transported to a time of old, the palace was a mixture of Cinderella's castle and Buckingham Palace all rolled into one, with subtle hints of desert culture included.

It was painted white, the perfect artist's backdrop for the colorful Moroccan shutters, some of them open and some closed, protecting the windows.

The staircase leading up to the palace entrance gleamed as if recently polished. Columns with various scroll designs and colors rose majestically, creating an open feeling without looking out of place.

So intent was she on her observations, Catherine was

startled when Samir opened her door and held a hand out to her.

"Thank you," she said.

"You're welcome. If you'll go up the stairs, I will bring your luggage. I'm sure the king and queen are anxious to meet you." He glanced toward the palace.

Standing on the landing, in the shade, were a man and a woman. Catherine smoothed down her skirt, praying it wasn't too wrinkled from her travels. She had hoped to freshen up before meeting her hosts, but how could she have known she'd be waylaid at the airport by a handsome stranger without time to duck into the ladies' room?

With a smile, she held her head high and walked up the steps. Heat rose from the ground with each step she took. It was going to take her a while to get used to the heat. London had been dreary and raining when she left.

"Miss Taylor," said the queen, holding out her hand. "I'm so glad you arrived."

Catherine was startled to hear a British accent. "Thank you, ma'am." She took the queen's hand and curtseyed. The queen's blond hair was pulled back into a neat bun, and she wore a caftan of white with red and gold stripes running through it. Catherine hadn't been aware the queen was British.

"None of that," laughed the queen. "Call me Anna. We're very informal people in our home."

With a nod, Catherine glanced at the man standing next to the queen. He wore dark pants with a white shirt, and his black hair was streaked with gray. "Sir," she said with a slight bow.

The man laughed, full and rich. "I'm Jamal. As my wife said, we're very informal, Miss Taylor." He frowned as he looked over her shoulder.

The queen's gaze widened. "Please, come inside out of this heat. Jamal will see to your luggage."

"Oh, but … "

"It will be my pleasure," the king said. "Especially since none of my sons are here at the moment. Plus, I'd like a word with Samir."

Catherine glanced over her shoulder to see Samir standing at the bottom of the stairs with her suitcase and carry-on bag at his feet. "I'm sure the driver will bring in the luggage, sir. And I still need to pay him." She started to turn away, but the queen captured her arm.

"Nonsense, my dear. Jamal will take care of the driver and your luggage."

"I most certainly will." The king's tone was stern, and Catherine couldn't help but watch over her shoulder as the queen escorted her to the entrance of the palace. The king and Samir were having a very animated discussion before her view was cut off.

She was tempted to intervene. She didn't want Samir to get into trouble just because the stranger at the airport had put her into his taxi, but the sudden coolness of the entryway made it easier for her to breathe. Then she lost her breath all together as she took in the entryway.

The high ceilings created an open feeling, but the colorful motifs captivated her attention. A variety of designs and patterns covered the walls. Each one was unique in color and style, and they painted a tableau of an alluring desert encampment. The artist in her wanted to study each and every one of them.

Anna led Catherine down a long corridor, past several doors and sets of guards, to a cozy room, decorated in neutral brown and beige colors. Sofas were scattered around the room, along with side tables. The main window took up one wall, ceiling to floor, allowing natural light to flood the room, yet the sheers and natural hedge outside allowed for privacy as well.

"Please have a seat," Anna said, gesturing to one of the sofas. "I think juice is in order, rather than tea." The queen looked at her for confirmation.

"Juice is fine." Catherine sat down on the sofa, feeling a bit out of place. While the space was welcoming, she was aware that most of her flat back home could fit into this room.

Within minutes a tray of juice with cookies was brought in by a servant. Catherine picked up her glass and sipped. The coolness of the liquid as it slipped down her dry throat gave instant relief.

"Jamal and I are so excited you have arrived." The queen smiled. "There was some, how can I put this, discussion with your manager about your coming to Bashir."

Catherine set her glass down, not realizing Bill had

expressed any concerns about the trip. "I'm sorry if I've caused you an inconvenience. It's rare that Bill agrees to any job without my input, Your Majesty. I had to rearrange some things in order to come to your lovely country."

She hoped she sounded sincere, because she was. Her objection to the job had more to do with personal reasons rather than professional. This was a high-profile job, and her run-in with the paparazzi reminded her of times she'd rather forget.

"No inconvenience on our part. I'm happy you were able to accommodate us. Now, tell me how you'd like to work while you're here."

Catherine wasn't sure how one could be informal with royalty, but there were some things she needed to know. "First, I hope my clothing is okay. My manager didn't give me a lot of information on the clothing requirements."

Anna smiled. "No worries, my dear. We are mainly a Christian country. There are some Muslims. For generations, both religions have worked side by side. You'll see both Western dress and Arab dress while you're here."

Catherine breathed a sigh of relief. Over the next half hour she explained to Anna how she'd like to view the room where the mural would go, and if possible, talk with the children who would be occupying the room.

Bill, her manager, had told her the king and queen had seen her work when it had been featured in a magazine and wanted her to paint the mural. She'd only agreed to the job when she'd been told the mural was for critically ill children at the new hospital. Otherwise, she would have made her manager turn down the high-profile job.

"That sounds doable. May I ask why you want to talk with the children?"

"To get their ideas. This isn't like painting a mural in the lobby of an office or for a city building. The children will be in this room for weeks or sometimes even months. Getting their input on what they'd like to see is invaluable."

Catherine paused. "I will need someone to translate while I'm here. I'm afraid I was only able to learn a little bit of Arabic before I left home."

"That won't be an issue. English is a common second language here. All the children are taught it."

"That's a relief. I was worried about how I would communicate with them."

"I can see now why you're so sought after. Not only do you have incredible talent, but you're also very compassionate and willing to listen."

"Thank you, Your Majesty." She gave a little smile when the queen raised her eyebrows. "Anna," she amended.

The queen gave a dainty laugh. "You're going to be very good for my family. I take it you had a good flight?"

"Yes, it was very smooth. I just had … " Catherine trailed off, not sure how much she should share with the queen. Before she could speak, a yawn escaped. "Oh, please excuse me." Another yawn escaped. Lord, how gauche could she be?

"No apologies. Traveling can be tiring." The queen

stood. "I'll show you to your room. I'm sure Jamal has already taken care of your luggage."

Catherine followed Anna up a set of stairs and past another set of guards. "I should explain," the queen said, gesturing to the guards. "I'll give you the grand tour later, but there are basically three levels. The basement houses security; the first level has our offices, official function rooms, and some family rooms; then this floor, which houses all our private rooms." The queen led Catherine down the hall. "The guards keep unwanted visitors from our private floor."

Anna paused at a door, then flung it open. "This is your room. I hope you will be comfortable here." She gestured for Catherine to enter.

"Oh, my," Catherine said as she moved into the room. It was huge. The balcony doors were open, and the warm, fresh air teased her senses.

On one side of the room there was a small bar area, complete with a coffeepot and sink. A small oak dining table with chairs occupied the space in front of the bar. Several sofas were spread around the room, each plush and inviting with an array of throw pillows. A full-size cherrywood desk and leather chair in the corner rounded out the furniture in the room.

"This could be considered a living room; the bedroom is beyond that door." The bracelets on the queen's wrists jingled when she waved her hand in the direction of the bedroom. "The bathroom is to the right. I instructed a maid to unpack your belongings." Anna smiled. "I'll leave you now to rest. I'll send a maid up an hour before dinner to allow you time to freshen up."

"Thank you." Catherine tried to wrap her mind around what was happening. She wasn't used to such luxury. It was a far cry from her earlier starving-artist days.

Anna paused by the door. "I'm hoping over dinner you can explain how Samir came to drive you home." Then she scooted out the door and closed it behind her.

Catherine pondered the queen's question until she walked into the bedroom. The four-poster canopy-top bed drove all thoughts from her mind. Draped in what looked like gauzy silk fabric of multiple colors, it dominated one full wall and was a bed out of a dream.

She yawned. Sleep, then she'd contemplate why the queen asked her about Samir. She shook her head. What a small country if royalty knows every taxi driver's name.

Several hours later, Catherine pulled back the heavy bedroom curtains, letting in the bright sunlight. She'd forgotten to ask the queen what time dinner was and a maid had yet to arrive. Glancing at her watch, she saw that it was barely past six, yet the sun was still very bright.

Without thought, she found her bag and pulled out her sketchpad, and sitting with crossed legs on the mattress, she began sketching—her first impression of the palace, the city, and lastly of the stranger at the airport.

She frowned at the drawing. It wasn't enough. While it looked like him, something was lacking. Tossing her sketchpad down, she padded over to the window.

The garden below called out to her, with its winding pathways and exotic plants. How did they keep it so lush in the desert climate? The greenery energized her soul. A little exercise wouldn't hurt. After slipping on her shoes and grabbing her sketchpad and pens, she left her room.

At the end of the hallway, she asked the guard how she could get to the garden. With a polite smile, he escorted her down another set of stairs. At her inquiry, he told her dinner would be at eight. He opened a door and explained she could use it to come back into the palace and to her room.

When she stepped outside, the scent of jasmine filled her senses and her muscles instantly relaxed. The quiet snick of the door closing spurred her into action. She took the first path until she found a nice grassy area beneath a palm tree. She sat and opened her sketchpad.

Her fingers flew over the pages as she captured the scenes flittering through her mind. She lost all track of time until a husky male voice said, "Hello, beautiful."

Her head snapped up to see the stranger from the airport.

3

Malik strolled through the palace, grateful no one was around. He needed some time alone, some time to digest what the prime minster had told him. Quietly, he made his way over the highly polished floors to the door that led to the gardens.

Once outside, he took a deep breath, inhaling the aromas of rose, jasmine, and frankincense. The sweet fragrances relieved some of his stress. The garden was his refuge when he needed to think or to get away from everyone. The peace and quiet were exactly what he needed before he had to face his family and their guest over dinner.

Malik blew out a breath. The prime minister was very encouraging of what Malik and his father hoped to accomplish, and while the prime minister was a little more progressive, he wasn't sure about upsetting his people. That news hadn't been what Malik had hoped for. They needed to bring their countries into the current century rather than living in the past; if they didn't, they were going to be left behind. They were getting better with exporting the food they grew, and wool, but there was always more they could do.

It was a wonder he'd been able to get through the meeting at all since that kiss with a certain female at the airport had distracted him. Her dark red hair had flowed over her shoulders, her skin had been as smooth as a rose petal, and those blue eyes … they reminded him of the water at the oasis by his desert encampment. Calm and cool. And her lips … full, soft, and very kissable.

A different type of tension filled him, but this time it was pleasurable. He hadn't reacted to a woman like that in years, and he couldn't say why he'd reacted that way to her. He didn't regret kissing her, he only regretted that the paparazzi had followed her and that he wouldn't be able to explore his attraction to her.

He needed to check with Samir about where he'd dropped her off, so he could at least send her a proper thank-you gift. He thought about maybe taking her the gift himself but nixed the idea. He didn't need a female complication right now, although it could be fun. Especially with a sexy British redhead.

He shook his head as he ambled down the path that led to the gazebo in the middle of the garden, when a flash of red glinting in the sunlight caught his eye. Stopping, he searched for the source.

It couldn't be. But unless his eyes were playing tricks on him, the woman from the airport was sitting under the big palm tree. Why had Samir brought her here? Had the paparazzi been that difficult? They shouldn't have been, not with his country's laws, but still guilt ate at him. He'd used her to take the press off his back, possibly making her life more difficult. It wasn't nice of him to do that to her, but what choice had he had at the time? His meeting with the prime minister of Shara was of the utmost importance, and it needed to be kept under wraps.

The woman's head was bent as she rapidly moved her hand over some sort of book. Her head moved up then back down again, and again, but her hand never hesitated. Was she sketching? His curiosity was aroused, along with other parts of his body. Maybe he would explore his attraction to her after all, show her his world.

Quietly, he moved toward her. He didn't want to startle her, but he hoped to see what she was drawing. The closer he got, the more his body reacted. Sensual heat filled him until he thought he'd burn up from the inside. He longed to repeat their kiss, except this time in private.

"Hello, beautiful," he said.

Her head came up and turned sharply in his direction. Her eyes widened when she saw him.

"What are you doing here?" she asked, pulling the sketchbook to her chest.

"I was about to ask you the same thing." He slipped closer. "What are you drawing?" He craned his neck but couldn't see anything.

"Nothing." She closed the book with a snap, but her cheeks turned pink, making him even more curious about what she'd been drawing.

Then a memory nudged his brain. "You're the artist commissioned to do the mural at the hospital." He shook his head, trying to reconcile her with the woman at the airport.

"Yes." Her chin came up, and he couldn't help but grin. She was defensive about her work for some reason. No worries; he thought it was great. But part of him wanted to haul her into his arms and kiss her again. Instead, he followed a saner choice and sat down on the grass across from her.

She wiggled an inch or two away, then her gaze met his. She was wary of him, but he caught a hint of curiosity in her gaze.

"I'm Catherine Taylor." She held a hand out to him.

"Malik." He grasped her hand, lowered his head, and caressed her knuckles with his lips. A slight shiver moved through her body and transferred to him. So she was affected by him. Good. He squeezed her fingers.

"Well, Malik, with no last name," she said, and tugged her hand away, "what brings you to the palace?"

He was taken aback, then realized she didn't know who he was and almost burst out laughing. It was rare he could be this anonymous.

"I was invited to dinner." While she'd eventually find out who he was, right now, he wanted to keep it a secret. Just be a normal guy and get to know her without his royal title being involved.

"Is it that late?" She lifted her wrist, and then shook her head. "I left my watch in my room."

"It's only seven. Dinner won't be for another hour." Now that he wasn't rushed for time, he allowed himself to look her over. Her long legs were tucked underneath her. The small vee of her shirt gave him a glimpse of her curves.

She regarded him with a bit of suspicion. "Do you have dinner here a lot?"

"Yes." He liked the way she reacted to him. Like a normal man and not the crown prince. It was a nice change. No scraping and bowing or kissing up for position for this woman, and he was enjoying every second of it. "Come." He rose to his knees and grasped her elbow. "Let me take you on a tour of the garden." He brought her to her feet as he rose.

"But—"

"Nothing." He pressed a finger against her lips and had to bite back a groan when her tongue touched the pad of that finger. "We have plenty of time before dinner, and I'm sure you'll enjoy the tour."

Catherine stared at the man. Confusion about him, as well as riotous feelings, ran through her body. He invoked desires she'd thought long buried. She should be running a thousand miles from him, but instead she allowed him to lead her around the gardens.

Thank goodness she'd left her closed sketchbook back where she'd been sitting. There was no sense in his seeing what she'd drawn there. It was too personal, too sensual to share with a man she barely knew. A man who screamed danger to her emotional side.

Oh, quit being dramatic, she told herself. It was unlikely this man was even aware of who she was or of her wild side. After a few minutes, she relaxed and enjoyed the tour. His knowledge of the garden was vast, from the cacti and succulents, to sweet acacia and oleanders, to tubular flowers, desert willows, and palm trees. She wondered if he was the gardener.

She glanced at his hands. No, there were no rough calluses scraping her skin at his touch. So who was he? He hadn't given her a single clue. But she was enjoying walking by his side and listening to his deep voice.

When they arrived back at the spot where he'd found her, she knelt and picked up her sketchpad. "I must go and get ready for dinner."

"Of course." He took her hand and pressed a kiss into her palm, and briefly the tip of his tongue swept over her skin, making her nerves dance. "Until later, my beautiful dove."

As he walked away, she thought about how easy it would be to let this man overwhelm her common sense. He was so naturally charismatic, he should be locked up before every woman within a hundred-mile radius fell in love with him.

Her stomach fluttered; that man was trouble. And she wasn't very good at avoiding danger. Look at what had happened with Jamie and the press, one unholy mess. With a sigh, Catherine turned and went inside. She'd treat Malik like a ship passing in the night, if only she could stop thinking about him.

As she arrived at her room, a maid showed up, advising her she had a half hour before dinner and asking if she needed any help getting ready.

Catherine declined the help and went into the bathroom. After a quick shower, she pulled an emerald sundress out of the closet. Nice enough but not too formal. Would Malik like it? She shook her head, reminding herself she was dressing for herself, not him. She applied a light coating of makeup and then gathered up her hair and secured it in an ornate clip Jamie had given her. Her fingers trembled. Jamie had bought the clip in Spain, on one of his road trips. Tears gathered in her eyes.

While the intense pain from losing him was gone, her memories of him were fully intact. He had been her best friend, and she missed him every day. She missed his wacky sense of humor, the way he'd make fun of himself, and especially the way he could make her laugh.

She sobered instantly. She hadn't laughed in a long time. Her stomach churned, knowing she didn't have a lot of laughter in her life. Well, that would change with this job.

Children had a way of making you laugh, because kids were kids no matter where you were in the world.

Shaking away her gloomy thoughts, Catherine slipped into a pair of black ballet slippers and left the room. She followed the maid's instructions to the staircase and descended.

Malik waited at the bottom of the stairs. Damn, if the man didn't look sexy. He was dressed a bit more formally than earlier, now in black slacks and a white shirt with a black jacket, but no tie.

His raven hair, which earlier had looked wild and untamed, now lay silky against his scalp, but she detected a wave flowing through it. She longed to run her fingers through his hair just to see how soft it really was.

"Good evening, Catherine." His husky greeting sent shivers of awareness skittering over her nerves.

"Good evening, Malik."

"You look stunning." He took her hand and pressed it against his chest, right over his heart.

His heart beat strong beneath her palm, while her heart pounded. She was glad she'd dressed up a little bit. "And I think you're a natural flirt." For some reason, the banter relaxed her. Usually, she didn't go in for teasing, but she enjoyed it with him.

"Guilty as charged." He leaned down. "But don't tell anyone or else I'm done for," he whispered before straightening and tucking her hand in the crook of his arm. "It is my pleasure to escort you."

"Lead on." She followed him down the same hallway she'd taken that morning with the queen, and into the same room.

Catherine wasn't sure what to expect, but the last thing she'd anticipated was the room to fall silent when they entered. All eyes were focused on them.

"It figures. The oldest always gets to the ladies first," said one of the men. Catherine sucked in a breath; he was a younger version of Malik.

"Oh, hush," Anna said, walking to them. "I hope you had a nice rest, Catherine."

"Yes, I did. Thank you." Catherine's gaze quickly went to the three men standing in the room whom she hadn't met. It was easy to see the resemblance among them all. Jet black hair, varying shades of brown eyes, and to top it off, they all had the same bone structure as the king. Including Malik. Her stomach clenched.

Was he part of the royal family? This gorgeous man who'd kissed her in the airport, was he royalty? Her muscles tightened as the conversation flowed around her, and she looked from face to face, seeing if she could figure out where Malik fit.

"At least my oldest son has some manners, compared to the rest of you," Jamal said as he crossed the room to the small bar.

"Oh, please. It's been drummed into him since he was two. Of course he has better manners than the rest of us. He's not human anymore," said another man with a drink in his hand, his dark hair slightly longer than that of the other men.

"Yeah, always minding his p's and q's. Thank goodness I didn't have to do that," said another. When Catherine glanced at him, she figured him to be the youngest. His features seemed slightly boyish as he rocked on his feet.

"Boys, please," Anna said, exasperation tinting her voice.

"What would you like to drink, Miss Taylor?" the king asked.

The question jolted her out of her study of each person. "Juice, if you have it, sir. And please call me Catherine."

The king smiled. "Of course, Catherine." He poured a glass of dark red liquid and brought it over to her. "And please remember, I'm Jamal."

Catherine took a sip of the cool pomegranate juice, then set the glass down upon hearing raised voices. Nearby, the three other men jostled for position.

Jamal let out a deep-throated laugh. "Let me introduce you to these boys before they fall over each other."

He took her arm away from Malik and led her across the room. "This is Rafi."

"Miss Catherine." Rafi took her hand and kissed the back of it. "I'm affectionately known as 'the spare'. If you want to ride in the desert, I'm your man."

The man next to Rafi gently removed her hand from his. "Rafi is a flirt. I'm Hassan. I'm a doctor at the hospital where you'll be painting the mural."

Catherine was briefly startled by Hassan's blue eyes. Everyone else had dark eyes. Hassan grinned. "I'm a throwback to an older generation, or so I'm told. Thank goodness there are paintings to prove it or everyone would think I was adopted."

She laughed. "I look forward to seeing them, and it's great you're the doctor. I look forward to working with you." These guys had cornered the market on charisma and charm.

"And I'm Khalid," the third man said, drawing her hand away from Hassan. "I take care of security. Which I can see will need to be beefed up since we now have a single, gorgeous woman at the palace."

Catherine's cheeks grew warm, but before she could say anything, Malik said, "Flirts, all of you."

He stared at each man as he spoke. "If she wants to ride in the desert, I will be taking her, Rafi. Hassan, you have better things to do at your hospital, so I will take care of Catherine. Khalid, put your charm in your back pocket where it belongs." His voice was hard, but there was a slight teasing note in it as well.

Everyone in the room burst out laughing, and it gave Catherine a chance to study each man again. Then it hit her. Her brain finally put together all the pieces of seeing the men in the family together. Now she couldn't miss the resemblance Malik had to the king, nor could she miss it with the other men.

"Boys," Anna said, clapping her hands together. The

room quieted. "We don't want to frighten Catherine away on her first night."

"That's quite all right, Anna." Catherine deliberately caught each man's gaze for a moment before coming to rest on Malik. "Boys will be boys, no matter what age." Then she asked, "And Malik, what's your position in the family?"

Silence fell on the room, then Rafi let loose with what she classified as a snort of laughter. He walked to where Catherine stood next to Malik.

Taking her hand, he placed it in Malik's. "Catherine, may I introduce you to Malik Jamal al-Hakim, the crown prince of Bashir."

Her fingers tightened around Malik's as the room spun. The crown prince, then that meant … oh, God. She'd kissed the future king.

Malik wanted to shoot his younger brother, but at the moment there was nothing he could do. He gazed at Catherine's face. At first he saw disbelief in her eyes, then acceptance, followed by anger before she masked it.

"I didn't realize." She tried to tug her hand away, but he refused to let her go.

"No reason to treat me any differently, no matter what my brothers say." He hoped she understood. He wanted her to treat him like she would any other man, and he would make that clear to her later. In private, away from his interfering family.

"Enough of this posturing," Jamal said, removing her hand from Malik's. "As the oldest male, it will be my pleasure to escort the two most beautiful women into dinner."

Catherine didn't look back as his father led her to the dining room. Malik clenched his jaw and followed.

Malik took his usual seat next to his father and watched Catherine. She was quiet during dinner, unless asked a direct question. Of course, his brothers made up for her silence.

It bothered Malik to see Catherine withdrawn. Admittedly, he didn't know her very well, but this quiet woman was at odds with the woman he'd met that afternoon, the vibrant woman who'd walked around the garden with him. The woman who'd kissed him at the airport.

He was glad when dinner was over and they were headed back to the living room. Now he could have a quick conversation with her. As everyone made their way into the room, Malik snagged Catherine by the arm and pulled her aside. "You're angry with me."

"Yes. Why did you kiss me?"

Malik considered her question. "Because I wanted to," he said truthfully. He always tried to be honest.

"Was it necessary to sic the paparazzi on me?"

He winced. "I'm sorry about that. I had no options to speak of. I was trying to accomplish a meeting. If the paparazzi got ahold of it, it would be front page news, and the idea would never see the light of day." He clenched his free hand. "I didn't want to use you that way, but when I saw you … "

He glanced up, and she turned her head. His family was in an animated discussion. He cupped her chin and brought her attention back to him. Malik lowered his voice and head.

"When I saw you, you were my angel coming to the rescue. The kiss wasn't planned, I couldn't help myself. Especially when you kissed me back." And what a kiss it had been. He wanted to taste her ruby lips once again, but he'd wait.

"Yes, well … " Catherine dipped her head away from his hold. "I don't go around kissing strangers."

"Of course you don't." He was intrigued by her pink cheeks. But she had no reason to be upset. He was the one whose actions were questionable. He cupped her chin again and raised her face so he could see into her eyes. "There is nothing to be embarrassed about. It was an honest kiss between two honest people. I'd rather have honesty than artifice any day."

"I'm sure you get a lot of it in your daily life." When he didn't answer, she went on, "Artifice, that is."

"More than I want."

A mutual silence fell between them. "I appreciate your getting the press off my back," Malik finally said.

"It's hard having to face them twenty-four seven," she said quietly.

"More than you know."

Catherine almost said she did know. Been there, done that type of thing. She'd had enough being the center of attention with the press because of her parents, and then with Jamie. Although it hadn't been Jamie's fault. But she wasn't going to mention any of this to Malik; she wanted to be known for herself and her work, not her family connections.

In some ways, she understood why Malik had done what he did with the press. It didn't mean she had to like it, but she understood it. Her anger evaporated. He had his reasons, even if he couldn't share them with her.

"How about a deal?" she asked.

"I'm listening." He leaned closer.

"You don't feed me to the press again, and I'll forgive you."

Malik grinned and her heart turned over. His sexy grin could tempt a nun to sin. Gentle fingers grasped hers, raising her hand and laying it over his heart. "I promise not to leave you alone with the press."

"Shouldn't you be holding your own hand over your heart?"

"I like yours better."

He was an unabashed flirt, and she'd better remember that. He was the crown prince, and she needed to remember that too. While, logically, she should be running a thousand miles away from him, emotionally, she couldn't. Something about him tugged at the place locked away in her heart, and if she were being honest with herself, she didn't want to run, at least not yet. She wanted to explore her feelings with Malik, no matter how dangerous it could be to her emotional health.

Those feelings could get her into big trouble. She was

treading a fine line here. Malik should be off limits to her, not only because he was the crown prince, but because of the press. They could be so relentless, and the last thing she wanted was them digging up her past. But for the moment, she was safe.

"Why don't we join the others?"

"Of course." Instead of releasing her as she expected, he kept her hand tucked in his, even after they were seated and coffee was being served.

When Catherine saw Rafi's questioning look, she slipped her hand away from Malik's. This was awkward. Yes, she wanted to get to know Malik better, but she wasn't ready for him to claim her as his.

"Are you planning to visit the hospital tomorrow?" Anna asked, ignoring the tension in the room.

"Oh, yes," Catherine said, grateful to Anna for returning to the topic of her work. "I can't wait to see where I'll be working." She was eager to start on the mural. It would take her mind off Malik and her thoughts about him. Nothing absorbed her attention more than creating art.

"Are you sure?" Jamal asked. "It's quite all right if you wish to wait a day or two until you're used to the heat."

"Thank you, Jamal, but I'll be fine," she assured him. The only time she'd be out in the heat was when she went outside, as most hospitals were air-conditioned.

Jamal kept his gaze on her for a moment, before turning to Malik. "Of course, Malik will be your escort, and he will explain everything we're hoping to accomplish with the mural."

"Wait a minute, that should be my job," Hassan said in a teasing tone. "After all, I'm the doctor and the mural was my idea."

"Rank has its privileges." Malik gave her another one of his heart-stopping grins. Her reaction to him was not good, and having him escort her around wasn't going to help. She didn't need to be around him any more than necessary.

Lord, she was a mass of contradictions. At first she had wanted to explore these new feelings with Malik, and now she didn't.

"As head of security, it should be my job," Khalid said.

Catherine watched as the brothers bantered back and forth about who should escort her and who would be better for the job. Except Rafi; he seemed content to let the others talk. When Rafi noticed she was looking at him, he winked.

Since she was an only child, she'd never been around a family like this. Her childhood had been spent either in front of the press or with a nanny, so to say she was fascinated by the byplay of the brothers was an understatement.

Jamal was also sitting this out, letting Malik, Hassan, and Khalid argue back and forth. Malik seemed to be winning, and she wondered if as a child he'd ordered his brothers around as he was trying to do now.

Anna clapped her hands and Catherine jumped. The room fell silent and all eyes turned to the queen. "I believe that Catherine should be allowed to decide who she wants to escort her."

Now all their gazes focused in on her, and she barely prevented a groan from escaping. The last thing she wanted was to be the center of attention. Yet she'd been thrown into the deep end without knowing how to swim.

Be diplomatic.

"I don't want to take anyone away from their work." What else could she say? That she preferred to be alone and not have an escort? While this was a progressive country, she was aware women were very much protected by their families.

"Since it's in Malik's job description to escort anyone visiting the royal household, the job is his," Jamal said in a stern tone.

"Oh, but—" Catherine stopped. What could she say? That she didn't want Malik escorting her because she was afraid of the feelings she had for him? Nope, that wouldn't work. Pasting a smile on her face, she said, "That's fine."

"Good, that's settled," Jamal said. "Now, shall we talk about something more interesting, like who is going to win the World Cup this year?"

Catherine breathed a sigh of relief, and her nerves settled down as attention was diverted from her, until Malik leaned over and whispered, "I can't wait to be alone with you."

Her blood pressure shot off the chart as her body went on high alert. This was not good, not good at all. Only a few whispered words from him and she wanted to melt into a puddle. She shifted slightly away from him.

She needed to escape. "Excuse me, all. I'm feeling a little tired, so I think I'll retire." Even to her ears it sounded like an excuse, but she needed to get out of the room and away from Malik. She had to rebuild her defenses before tomorrow morning, or she'd be in real trouble.

Malik was the crown prince, she was a nobody, but it was more than that. She was positive the press followed him around like a hound dog on the scent trail, and she didn't want to deal with reporters or their invasive questions. No, it was better to nip this in the bud before it even began.

"Of course," Anna said. "Sleep well." Everyone but Anna stood as she rose and walked out of the room. It only took her a few minutes to arrive at her room, if one could call it that. It was more like a small apartment.

In the living room, she began to pace. What was she going to do? Her blood heated every time she was with Malik in ways it hadn't done in years, and it wasn't as if she'd lived like a nun. She'd dated since Jamie, but none of those men had affected her this way.

Enough; she needed to put Malik out of her mind. She could deal, didn't she always? Oh, but sometimes she wished she didn't have to. She'd love to just let go and not worry about how she was going to be viewed.

Wait, she'd done that once, and it hadn't worked out so well. Catherine picked up her cell phone and checked the time. Ten at night here in Bashir and eight in London; good. She pulled up her contacts and hit the call button.

"Catherine!"

"Hey, Sara." She was so happy to hear her best friend's voice.

"How's it going?" Sara's voice was bubbly.

"Good. I … " Catherine shook her head.

"Something is up, you've only been in the country barely a day. What's going on?"

"You'd better get comfy."

"Already done. I got off shift at four today, so I've been home for a while."

"Oh, that's good." Sara was a nurse and sometimes worked crazy hours.

"So, tell me, how is the royal family? Anything like ours?"

Catherine laughed. "They're very easygoing and friendly. Not that the British royal family wouldn't be, but … I don't know, they're different. I think it helps that the queen is British."

"Ohhh, that's nice. So what about the princes? Are they handsome?"

"Handsome, hot, and sexy." Awareness slid through her veins. "The crown prince especially."

"Now, that sounds interesting, tell me more about him."

"Malik is sexy, flirty and … he kissed me." Heat warmed her face.

"Already, damn, he moves fast."

"It's not like that." Catherine told Sara all about the meeting at the airport, the kiss, the press, and meeting back at the palace.

"How are you dealing with the paparazzi?" Sara was well aware of her aversion to the press.

"Not well. But, Sara, he's the crown prince, I shouldn't be lusting after him."

"Why the hell not?" Sara's voice held a note of irritation.

"I don't need a high-profile relationship. This job is high-profile enough."

"I've said this before and I'll say it again, your past is your past. Let it go and move on with your life. Nothing is going to change if you don't."

Catherine sighed. "I honestly know that, but making it a reality is really difficult at times." She rubbed her forehead. "How are things going at the hospital? Are you still having trouble with that one doctor?"

"I'm not the only one."

Thirty minutes later, Catherine hit the end button on her phone, feeling better. Her talks with Sara always made her feel that way. Catherine made her way into the bedroom and changed into her nightshirt, then fell onto the mattress. But instead of falling asleep, she lay there reliving the kiss at the airport and the feelings it awoke. She turned over and over again. After an hour, she gave up, climbed out of bed, and pulled on her robe.

Why couldn't she get Malik and his kiss out of her head?

The feel of his lips against hers lingered, and the subtle taste of mint teased her tongue. It wasn't fair. Crossing the room, she flung open the French doors and stepped out onto the balcony.

The night air was warm and carried the scents of jasmine and plumeria. She made her way to the railing and gazed out at the garden and courtyard below. Beyond that was the desert.

What would it be like to ride out there? How had it been years ago when the land was untamed? Her mind turned to history, thinking of the Bedouin people wandering the desert, and within minutes she was lost in her thoughts.

She didn't know how long she stood there, but finally a sense of peace came over her. Maybe now she could sleep.

She turned and froze.

Malik leaned against the balcony railing, watching her. When their gazes met, a frisson of heat slipped up her spine, and her nipples tightened.

The instant she spotted him, surprise lit up Catherine's eyes, which was Malik's intent, and it pleased him. But then, instead of pleasure, her expression turned to tension. Disappointment knifed him in the chest. He'd have to change her reaction to him, and fast. Admittedly, he'd been watching her for a while, making no attempt to conceal himself, but not wanting his presence known either.

He enjoyed observing her undisturbed. She'd been totally oblivious to his presence, and it had allowed him the privacy to study her, to enjoy her as a regular man, without the usual considerations normally expected of him.

And he liked it. Liked being able to observe her uninterrupted. Maybe it was more, like how unguarded she was. She'd been lost in thought, staring out at the desert, and for the first time since he'd met her, she'd looked at peace.

Of course, the way her robe hugged her body made him want to trace those subtle curves with his hands. Slowly push the robe off her shoulders and caress her silky skin. Would her nipples pucker? Were they a dusky rose color or more like ripe strawberries?

Malik sobered at the thought. She was a guest and should be treated with respect. Hospitality was in some ways the strictest protocol of his culture. Everyone from the humblest desert nomad to the king observed the ancient traditions of treating a guest with the highest honor.

Even as part of him recognized this fact, another part continually relived their kiss at the airport. While he was kissing her, he'd been merely a man, not the crown prince, but a man enjoying a kiss with a beautiful woman. And he wanted more. More of her kisses, more of her. All of her.

"I didn't realize anyone was out here," she said.

Malik pushed away from the railing. "I should apologize for disturbing you." She shivered as he stepped closer. "Are you cold?" He frowned.

The night air was warm to him, but that didn't mean it was to her.

"No." But her body shook again.

If she wasn't cold, what was making her shiver? Her breath grew shallow and her eyes larger. His gaze swept over her body. Her nipples were pressing against the fabric of her robe in hard little peaks. She was aroused. She was shivering from excitement, not cold. He hid a smile. She wasn't as unaffected as she'd like him to believe.

"I didn't mean to make you uncomfortable tonight." He was taking a shot in the dark, but his mother had chastised him for flirting with Catherine, possibly causing her to retire early.

Catherine shrugged and her robe slipped, giving him a peek at her creamy skin. His groin tightened as he found himself without the right words. A first for him. He usually knew exactly what to say to a woman.

"You're different from other women." He stepped closer to her.

"In what way?" Her back stiffened. Damn, she misunderstood him. "Well?" she asked, tilting her head to the side while staring at him.

He barely resisted the urge to plant kisses along her exposed neck. His forefathers had the right idea when one of them saw a woman he wanted—capture her, carry her off to his desert tent, and make her his. He drew in a deep breath. He needed to soothe over the nerves he'd bristled with his words, and then he'd go about wooing her.

He held up his hands in mock surrender. "You treat me like a regular man, not the crown prince, not the future king."

Her eyes softened. "Go on."

The struggle to find the right words frustrated him. "Usually, people are so concerned about offending the crown prince, they forget there is a living, breathing man beneath all the trappings."

"A man who would prefer people treated him as they would anyone else instead of the crown prince."

Her insight shocked him, but it was true. "You understand?" The answer was in her kind eyes. A sense of relief and satisfaction at being understood filled him.

"Yes." A cloud passed over her features, as if she remembered something unpleasant. Then it was gone. He was about to ask her about it when she resumed talking.

"But you are the crown prince and people look up to you. They want to be like you. They put their hope in you."

Maybe she didn't understand completely; disappointment scraped over his skin. "Yes, people do look up to me, but they also forget the man beneath. A man who has the same wants, hopes, and dreams as any other man."

He was close enough to her now that the heat of her body transferred to his. The subtle scent of vanilla tickled his nose. Ignoring the warning echoing in his head, he maneuvered his body around so her back was to the railing.

"Malik," she said, as she pressed her palms against his chest.

He stifled the urge to close his eyes in bliss at her touch. His heart thumped and his blood hummed in excitement at her nearness. A woman had never affected him like this, and he wasn't sure if it was a good thing or not. But right now he didn't care. "You are so beautiful," he whispered. He traced his fingers over her face, from temple to jaw, before dipping and exploring her throat. Her neck arched, allowing his questing fingers to continue their journey.

He'd been right. Her skin was silky smooth. He detested having to leave the delicious satin of her skin when the pads of his fingers met her robe. He slid his hands over her arms and past her fingers until his palms framed her hips. He frowned.

She was daintier than he'd realized. He would take care when he took her to bed, and maybe even more. His blood heated thinking about having Catherine in his bed, possibly spread-eagle, waiting for him.

"So beautiful," he whispered before lowering his head.

She opened her mouth and relaxed into his body when their lips touched. Ambrosia. And he needed … no, wanted more. He ran his tongue over her moist lips before slipping inside for a proper taste.

Her arms crept up around his neck as his tongue played with hers. Touching, entwining together before retreating. She tangled her fingers in his hair as he encircled her waist, pulling her tight against him as he deepened the kiss.

Their tongues played with each other as his fingers spread out over her butt. She was small, but he enjoyed the feel of her in his arms. His body grew tight and hard thinking about how she'd look once he stripped her clothing from her. His cock jumped.

Catherine stiffened and broke away from the kiss. Malik gazed down at her flushed face and dreamy eyes. She was aroused; good. He wanted her that way. He buried his face in her hair. Lemons. Her hair smelled of lemons.

Nudging his way past her tresses flowing around her

shoulders, he found the nape of her neck. He kissed it softly, before allowing his tongue to take a taste.

"Malik." Her voice was husky, and she wiggled in his embrace.

"You're delicious," he said against her neck before again swiping his tongue over her peachy-tasting skin. His lips skimmed up to her ear, and his teeth tugged on the lobe, before pulling it into his mouth to soothe the tiny bite with his tongue.

Her body trembled against his as her hands slid from his hair to his shoulders. She pushed against him. With a silent sigh, Malik raised his head to look at her flushed face.

"We shouldn't be doing this," she said.

"Why not?" Her eyes were bright with passion and something else—fear? Was she afraid of him? Impossible. But another side of his brain kicked in, reminding him that she didn't know him. While he would never harm a woman, her caution was warranted.

With great effort, he reined in his libido and stepped back, releasing his hold on her. His body protested, but he ignored it. "Catherine," he started.

She shook her head, and with a whispered, "I'm sorry," she darted around him and into her room. The doors clicked shut, and the snap of the lock seemed harsh in the night air.

Malik stood there, trying to rationalize what had happened, but it wasn't working. Women never ran from him. Ever. What had frightened Catherine so much that she needed to flee?

As he made his way back to his room, he tried to analyze her reactions. Had some man hurt her? His fingers clenched. The fear in her eyes was real. But what they'd shared on the balcony was special and something he'd like to do again.

Upon entering his room, he stripped and headed for the shower. Right now he needed to cool off, and the sooner the better. How many cold showers would be in his future as he continued to spend time with Catherine?

The icy spray chilled his body, but not his mind. There was something he couldn't name about Catherine that made him lose all rational thought. Made him want to do crazy things, like kissing her until neither of them could breathe, or carrying her off on his horse into the desert and shackling her to his bed to have his way with her. To make her cry with pleasure, lots of pleasure.

He let out a groan as his cock flexed against his body. Never had a woman gotten under his skin this quickly, and at a time when he should be concentrating on his country. Tomorrow he'd find out why she was frightened of what had happened tonight, because he couldn't stand the thought of her being scared of him.

But right now he had a more urgent need to take care of. He fisted his dick and began pumping. He needed some relief or he'd never sleep tonight.

Catherine stood inside the doors of her room, shivering until she heard Malik's footsteps fade.

What had she done? Mortification filled her. She wasn't a tease. Yet she'd barely known Malik a day and she was ready to jump into bed with him.

Another shiver worked its way up her spine. Would Malik take charge in the bedroom? Somehow she couldn't see him not. It had been a long while since she'd wanted a man to take control of her in bed. But Malik hit all her buttons. His clean masculine scent teased her senses, and the impression of his erection branded her.

From that brief encounter, she could tell he wasn't a small man. Oh, my, she tried to slow her breathing as she crossed the room and grabbed her sketchpad and pencil before shedding her robe and climbing back into bed.

Within minutes, she'd sketched Malik, shirtless, in leather pants, holding a flogger with a sexy, dominant smile on his lips. Oh, hell. She closed the pad and set it and the pencil on the nightstand.

It couldn't happen. She flipped off the light and snuggled under the covers. She was here to work, not have a kinky affair with the crown prince. Even if he was interested. And what about the press? Oh, Lord, if they got a hold of this, she didn't think she'd survive it this time. With Jamie it had been bad enough, with Malik … a disaster of biblical proportions.

Yet she understood his request about being seen as a man. How many times as a child had she wished people would see her for who she was, not who her parents were? Even as a teenager, the attention had never stopped. She'd been so happy to leave that life behind her.

Then there was Jamie. A sad smile crossed her lips. Jamie, her free-spirited, loving friend. Oh, so many of the press thought they were a couple, but Jamie was nothing but her best friend. She missed him so much. He'd been the one person she could really talk to, and he wouldn't judge her or tell her she was a failure.

Catherine sighed. Going over old ground wasn't going to help her. Tomorrow she'd keep things on a professional level, even if it killed her.

6

The next morning, Catherine grimaced at her reflection. She'd tossed and turned the rest of the night, her dreams filled with a kinky Malik. She didn't have a clue what she was going to do. Sometime during the endless night, she'd admitted to herself she stood no chance against her attraction to him, and he was a complication she didn't need. She was here to do a job, attraction or not.

Using makeup to hide the dark circles under her eyes, she gave her wardrobe the once over. She finally selected a pair of black jeans and a green blouse. Glancing at the clock, she saw it was after nine; she'd better hurry if she wanted something to eat before she left for the hospital.

Catherine made her way downstairs and headed for the dining room. But it was empty. Had she missed breakfast?

"May I help you, ma'am?"

Catherine jumped at the voice behind her and turned to see a maid giving her a timid smile.

"Did I miss breakfast?"

"No, ma'am. Everyone is in the breakfast room. This way." The maid gestured for Catherine to follow her.

She heard raised voices before she reached the door. "Thank you." She smiled at the maid, who scurried off. Catherine hovered in the doorway. There were people everywhere, or at least it seemed that way. Anna sat at the table, while Malik and his father were surrounded by a group of men, all talking at once. About to back away, she caught Anna's gaze the second the queen looked up. Anna motioned for her to enter.

The moment she stepped into the room, several pairs of eyes focused on her. She fought against the need to run. She hated being the center of attention like this. Stay calm. She forced her feet to move. At the table, she sat down, praying her hands would stop shaking. The conversation continued, all in Arabic.

"Good morning. Did you sleep well?" Anna asked; her voice was soft, but her eyes were filled with concern.

"Yes, I did, thank you," Catherine lied, as she reached for the coffee pot and poured a cup.

"Good," the queen said, studying her.

Catherine hoped the queen didn't see through her lie. Then the voices in the room grew louder, and Catherine glanced over at Malik, who was staring at her. Her spine stiffened and she returned his look. His dark eyes held a promise he'd finish what he'd started last night.

Molten heat invaded her veins. She hated that a single glance from him sent her emotions flaring out of control. In the past years, she'd fought to gain control over her emotions, and he wiped it all away with one heated glance. It was annoying, yet her tummy fluttered with anticipation.

The man nearest to Malik gestured in her direction, but Malik shook his head. Catherine dropped her gaze to the plate of toast and fruit set in front of her. But that diversion only lasted for a second, as her gaze was drawn back to Malik as if compelled by his continued regard.

Now several of the men gestured in her direction, and her belly clenched with unease. Why were they waving at her? Her stomach turned over. Something was going on and it involved her.

"Has something happened?" she asked Anna.

"You could say that," Anna said, her gaze appraising Catherine.

The cryptic answer annoyed Catherine, but before she could question Anna more, Anna turned her attention to her son and said something in Arabic.

Catherine silently cursed she hadn't had time to learn more than a few basic words. She transferred her glance from Anna to Malik.

A grin tugged at his lips, and her annoyance level rose. She clenched her hand beneath the table. "Would someone please tell me what is going on?" Damn, did she just blurt that out? Silence descended on the room. Yep, she did. Oh, this was not good. Malik rose from his seat, and the men around him melted away as he came to her side.

Her heart stopped. Had someone found out about her and Jamie? Or about her parents? Is that why everyone was upset? She pushed her plate away.

"This is my fault, not yours," Malik said, taking the empty seat next to her.

"What ... " She had to swallow before she could continue. "What is your fault?"

He gestured to the men standing in a huddle across the room. "My ministers are a little disturbed this morning."

"I would say it's more than that." She shivered at not only the hostile gazes focused in on her, but their stiff postures.

"You're right." He scooted his chair closer to her and took her hand. "But don't let them get to you. I'm taking full responsibility for what happened."

She signed in frustration. "Would you spit it out?"

"You're not going to like it."

"I didn't ask if I'd like it or not, just tell me. I don't need protecting." The longer he held off telling her, the worse it was in her mind. Was her job over before it had even started?

Malik glanced at his mother, who pushed several newspapers over to him. "I think these will give you the idea."

Catherine picked up the first paper and looked at it.

"Oh, dear God." The room spun. This was even worse than she'd imagined.

In full color on the front page was a picture of her and Malik kissing at the airport. The caption read, "The Crown Prince's Newest Woman." She flipped from one paper to the next. The paparazzi had done their job, and, as always, got it totally wrong. Each headline was different, and progressively worse, from "Crown Prince's British Mistress" to "Royal Family Secret Bride" to "Royal Baby Maker." There were several other pictures of her outside the airport and a few of her in the car.

Her hands shook. Oh, yes, this was far worse than her imagination, and that was saying something. She hated the paparazzi with a passion, and right now she wanted nothing more than to scream at the unfairness of it all, but she couldn't.

She wouldn't lose control. She'd learned her lesson after losing her control after Jamie died. Her anger and tears could wait until she was alone. Setting the papers on the table, she looked at the queen.

Compassion filled Anna's eyes. "I'm sorry, Catherine. The press has no right to invade your life like this."

"It isn't the first time," she whispered, unable to keep the bitterness from her voice. Once again the fates seemed to want her to suffer. She would survive, yet again. Anna opened her mouth, but several of the ministers burst into a heated discussion.

Catherine wanted to shrink away, to hide from everyone

and everything. But that wouldn't work as it had in the past few years. "I'll pack and be gone within the hour, if you could have someone make arrangements for a flight," she told Anna.

Her stomach tightened the second the words left her mouth. She was letting so many people down—her manager, the hospital, the kids, the king and queen, Malik— but she didn't have much of a choice.

"Like hell you will," said Malik, his expression fierce.

"I can't stay." Catherine bowed her head, fighting the tears filling her eyes. How long before the paparazzi dug up information on her parents and Jamie? She'd never regretted her time with Jamie, only how she'd reacted after his death when cornered by the press.

"Enough," Malik roared, rising to his feet. Catherine jumped at his abrupt action. "Out, everyone, except family and Catherine."

Within minutes the room was blissfully quiet. Catherine kept her head down. This was so unfair, but then so was life. She couldn't change what she'd done in the past with the press, no matter how much it affected her future.

Malik reclaimed his seat next to her, and then his warm fingers closed over her arm. She wanted to close her eyes and sink into his warmth; instead, she bit her lip as he cupped her chin and lifted it up.

"You are not leaving. I won't let you. None of this is your fault."

Malik watched Catherine closely. Her face was so pale

he was afraid she was going to faint and her eyes … He saw the tears she refused to shed.

Guilt punched him in the stomach. His last relationship had failed because of the press, and this one was headed in the same direction before it even started. He'd promised he'd never allow the press to hurt a woman in his life again, but damn if it hadn't happened. It was entirely his fault; he was the one who'd used her to distract the press at the airport.

The least he should have done was made sure no one captured a picture of her. But he'd been so wrapped up in his reaction to Catherine and his duty that he'd let everything else slip away. Now he had to live with the fallout. And so did she.

When she said she was leaving … He wouldn't allow that to happen. Without his protection the paparazzi would eat her alive.

"I meant what I said." He kept his voice even. While he was angry, it wasn't with her. "This is my fault."

"I think we both knew what would happen," she said quietly.

"I did," he corrected. "You had no idea the paparazzi would follow you like they did. I was counting on it, and I'm sorry I used you in that way. It was unworthy of me." And it was, as his mother had reminded him when she'd scolded him before Catherine had entered the room. Now, he had to pay for it. He didn't mind, but he wasn't going to let Catherine pay as well. It wasn't fair to her.

"Darn right it was," Anna said. "My firstborn son should know better."

Malik's lips twitched. His mother was angry with him and he understood why. He could handle her anger; he was good at it.

"Let's stick to the issue at hand," Jamal said for the first time.

His father had taken on the role as mediator with the council. "Yes." Malik took Catherine's hand in his and frowned at how cold it was. "We have to feed the press something."

Anna made a rude noise, and Catherine turned her head. "It seems my son has placed you in a very awkward position."

"Not just Malik," Jamal added. "I instructed him to avoid the press as much as possible, so I'm as much to blame as Malik. I'll accept my responsibility as well." He looked at Catherine. "You'll need protection."

"From what? The press?" Confusion crossed her features.

"Everyone," Malik muttered, and he waited until her gaze connected with his before continuing. "Protection from the press, from the world." The council and his enemies, he thought.

"I can take care of myself." She withdrew her hand from his and straightened her shoulders.

The fire in her eyes returned, and Malik was grateful. "Not if my ministers have their way."

"What do you mean?"

"They want me—"

"Absolutely not," Anna interrupted. "It's not fair to ask *that* of Catherine."

"What?" she asked.

Malik kept his gaze on Catherine and she held his stare. This woman wasn't the fragile flower he'd first thought. There was steel in her as well, and it was a good thing; she'd need it if things progressed. Maybe his ministers' idea wasn't all that bad. It would give him and Catherine time together to explore their attraction.

"Malik?" Catherine prompted, her arms crossed over her chest.

He took a deep breath. "My ministers want you to pretend the papers are right. That you are going to be my crown princess."

Two words echoed in her head. *Crown princess.* She closed her eyes, trying not to hyperventilate. The paparazzi would have a field day. They'd search and find her past, and she wouldn't, couldn't let that happen, not again. And if it did, how would it affect the royal family? She had to protect them at all costs—and herself.

The idea of playing along with a fake engagement? She couldn't. The paparazzi were not to be toyed with and neither were her emotions. Especially when Malik stirred her up like no other.

"No, I can't," she whispered as she fluttered her hands in the air.

Malik captured one hand and tightened his fingers around it until she looked at him. The concern in his gaze made everything fade away except the feel of his skin against hers.

She soaked up his warmth and marveled that for once she wasn't alone. There was someone fighting in her corner with her—for her.

"I understand." But his voice was flat, as if he were disappointed in her.

What did he expect? That she'd jump at the chance? Probably. What normal woman wouldn't want to be the crown princess? But all it did was remind her that she was different from most women, and the thought depressed her. She wanted to fit in or to at least be unnoticeable, not that it ever worked.

"Do you really?" she said softly, then her voice rose, "I'm not press material."

"Nonsense," Jamal said, gesturing at the photos in the papers. "You're very photogenic."

Catherine's lips twitched. Jamal had misunderstood.

"Photogenic or not, she has refused, my husband," Anna said. "And that is her decision. Let's talk with the ministers and see what we can do to get them to understand that Malik being seen with a British citizen, and kissing her, doesn't mean they're an item."

"Like we did with you?" Jamal let out a laugh. "You do know how that worked out."

"Hush, husband." Anna rose; then, arm in arm, Anna and Jamal left the room.

Catherine shook her head and then realized Malik was sitting there holding her hand. Why?

"My father is right, you're very photogenic." He rubbed his thumb over the back of her hand, causing little sparks to flow through her veins.

"You can't convince me to do this, Malik." She couldn't do it. The paparazzi would focus on her and her life, and she wouldn't go through that again. The wounds from Jamie were just beginning to heal. To do this would start the bleeding all over again.

Her best bet was to pack and hightail it back to London. At least at home she could lose the paparazzi. They'd give up the story after a few days, and she could go back to being a lonely artist. Oh, but she wanted to stay and do the mural. She wanted to make the children at the hospital happy and as carefree as she could with her art. She couldn't do that if she ran.

"Convincing you to do something you don't wish to do is the last thing on my mind." His gaze was intent on her, and Catherine couldn't help the feeling of caution slipping up her spine. "But you do realize you cannot leave Bashir."

"What?" She blinked. She had to leave, didn't he understand that? Especially now. Panic filled her stomach. Was she to become a prisoner in a gilded cage? She'd barely survived being one with her parents.

"Since we've been linked together, the press will follow you no matter where you go. Your best bet is to stay here where we—I—can protect you." He squeezed her fingers. "I promised you, you'd never have to face them alone, and I'm keeping that promise."

"But ... " Catherine shook her head. This was rapidly getting out of control, like a runaway boulder down a steep hill, and she wasn't sure if she could get out of the way before she was flattened.

"There is no 'but' allowed." Malik leaned forward, and she breathed in the scent of sandalwood. "They will follow you back to England and make your life a living hell. Here, I can protect you, keep them a safe distance away, and make sure you're never alone."

"That won't stop them." Part of her wanted to fling her arms around Malik and agree to anything he had to say. Outside of Jamie, no one had ever tried to protect her this way. Yet the other side of her reminded her she'd weathered storms like this before. She'd gotten through them by herself.

"No, but it will keep them at bay. I will have my minister of information release to the press that you are the artist who is here to paint the mural. Our meeting at the airport was planned, and I greeted you with a little more enthusiasm than normal. You are a friend of the royal family, nothing more."

"Like they're going to buy that. You kissed me." Now, why did she have to say that? She didn't need to be reminded of their explosive kiss. She needed a distraction. With her free hand, she gestured toward the papers still on the table, knowing she was trapped. The panic had died down, mainly because Malik's presence was keeping her sane.

"What they believe or not, I cannot do anything about." He framed her face with his palms, and his warmth seeped into her pores. "I can do nothing about what happened at the airport, except apologize for using you to distract the press. While I had my reasons for doing it, it was wrong, and I knew it." His thumb caressed her cheek in a soothing motion, while the look in his eyes begged her forgiveness.

All the anger and helplessness flowed out of her. This strong man was apologizing to her. Apparently, he'd had a good reason, even if he hadn't shared it, for having the press follow her. She took a chance and said, "You were trying to help your country, and I was needed to run interference."

"Yes." His soft breath caressed her skin. "But that doesn't excuse what I did. I take full blame for it, and I will do what I can to make it better, but I need your cooperation."

"You're doing this for a good cause, right? Not just some silly political gain."

"It's for my people."

A lump formed in her throat. He was trying to do good for his people and his country. "I don't know if I can help." How long would it take before the press dug up her past, even if Jamie had died seven years ago? What would happen then? How much of this would affect Malik? His family? His faith in her? His country? Let alone the effect on her emotions of being involved with Malik and this temporary engagement.

"At least think it over."

Disappointment shone in his eyes, but Catherine couldn't do anything about it. She had to protect herself. "I will."

"That's all I can ask." He slid his palms to her shoulders, grasping them lightly. "Hassan is expecting us at the hospital so you can look over the area where you'll be working. Let's hold any decision until after that."

"There are things you don't know about me, Malik." She had to make sure he understood, even if she didn't tell him fully about her life.

"I'm sure there are, and we have plenty of time to explore them. What's important right now is your being able to work without interference from the press."

He made things sound so simple, and probably from his perspective they were. Right now, she would go with the flow and keep a low profile. Her goal was to do the mural and leave; she had to keep that in mind. Regardless of the spark between her and Malik. "Okay, let's go see where I'll be working."

"That's my woman." He brushed his lips over hers, then pulled back. The contact made her skin tingle. "And I'll behave myself in public, I promise." He stood and held his hand out to her.

"Why doesn't that statement reassure me?" She allowed him to pull her to her feet. As brief as the kiss was, she wanted more. Not a good sign—she wanted to sink into his kiss, to feel his body against hers, to explore this attraction.

"Maybe because when we're alone, I make no promises." He gave her a wicked grin, his eyes alight with mischief. Her body tightened. "You see, Catherine, I find myself in a unique position."

"I know I'm going to regret this, but what position is that?"

His grin grew wider, and he said, "I want you."

She stared at him, barely breathing. He wanted her? "That's impossible," she blurted out. He couldn't be serious. Then she remembered the kiss on the balcony, the walk in the garden. Given the unadulterated desire she experienced with him, maybe it wasn't so impossible.

"I assure you, I do want you." He guided her out of the breakfast room and down the hall. "We will discuss my need for you later, too."

Malik led her out to the waiting vehicle. Her bag, with all her materials, was already there. She slid onto the supple leather seat, her mind still swirling over his wanting her. With a sigh, she closed her eyes and leaned her head back.

Didn't he get it? He couldn't want her. No one wanted her because she enjoyed a little kink in the bedroom. But if Malik did … she'd have no defenses against him. She didn't want to destroy his life. Oh, Lord, what was she going to do now?

She couldn't think, not about Malik and sex. Her core tightened with the knowledge that he wanted her. Her brain knew it was an impossible situation. Her heart craved a strong man who would take control in the bedroom. Her thoughts chased each other around, and by the time she and Malik had arrived at the hospital, she was no closer to a solution.

Her eyes opened to see people crowd around the vehicle the second it stopped. Paparazzi and what she assumed was security, based on their uniforms.

Malik swore. "How the hell did they know we were going to be here?"

"This is why I should leave. You don't need this." Her stomach tumbled over and over.

"I can handle them. I've been doing it since I was a kid. You, on the other hand, need protection. Don't answer them, keep your head held high, and walk straight into the building with me."

Catherine almost told Malik she didn't need tips on how to handle the press. Seven years had passed since she'd been under such scrutiny, but there were some lessons one never forgot.

One of the lessons she'd learned on the night Jamie died was not to duck and run. So many accusations had been thrown at her that night as she left the hospital. She hadn't even had time to process her grief over losing Jamie before the paparazzi had descended. Fear crawled into her throat.

"Ready?" Malik asked, bringing her out of her thoughts.

She took a deep breath. She could, no, would do this.

She wouldn't let Malik, his family, or the hospital's children down. "Let's go."

"That's my woman," he said again. *His woman.* What did that mean? Her stomach fluttered with the idea of being his woman. Malik raised his hand and the door was opened. He stepped from the vehicle and held his hand out to her. Grasping it, she allowed him to help her out.

Camera flashes went off, and she fought the urge to duck her head and hide behind Malik. No. She stood up straighter. She wasn't going to allow the press to threaten the inner peace she'd fought for years to achieve. She was strong. She could do this.

Lifting her chin, she kept pace with Malik as he guided her into the hospital, ignoring the shouts and flashes. She was grateful for Malik's strong presence by her side. Once inside the hospital, the noise from outside was muted, and Catherine breathed a sigh of relief.

"Very good." Malik brushed a kiss over her cheek, leaving a trail of fire. "You handled them like a pro. My personal security will take you to Hassan, and he will show you where you'll be working. I'll be there after I talk to the press."

"But," she protested, and caught his hand before he could turn away, "I haven't decided."

"Yes, you have. You made the decision by coming to the hospital with me."

Her mouth dropped open. She had done no such thing.

Perturbed, she crossed her arms over her chest and glared at him. "I came because I have a job to do."

"You could have walked away." His eyes gleamed in satisfaction.

"No, I have a contract and made a commitment to your family to paint the mural." Throwing a hand up, Catherine blew out a breath. "Besides, wasn't it you who said I couldn't leave Bashir?"

He inclined his head. "Because the press would follow you back to your country."

"And they're not following me now?" She wrapped her arms around her waist, staring at him.

"But I'm here to protect you." He grinned and ran a finger over her cheek, causing a delicious sensation of excitement to run though her body before he turned and walked away.

"This way, Miss Taylor." She recognized the voice. Catherine looked up to see the taxi driver from yesterday.

Lord, was it just yesterday? So much had happened since she'd arrived. It felt like weeks had passed.

"Samir?" she asked, as she fell into step with him.

"Yes, Miss Taylor. Prince Malik has asked me to become your personal bodyguard while you are here."

"But ... " Her mind tried to work out what Samir was saying. "You're not a taxi driver, are you?"

"No, my lady." He rubbed his ear. "King Jamal was not happy with me about the deception yesterday."

She remembered how the guard at the gate had reacted and then Jamal's animated conversation with Samir.

"Catherine," Hassan said, approaching the pair. "I'm so glad you decided to stay." He took her hand and kissed the back of it.

Samir cleared his throat, and Hassan smiled. "Relax, Samir, I'm family, after all." Hassan slid her arm through his. "Let me show you around."

An hour later, Catherine was much more relaxed. Hassan was an easygoing type of guy, and his passion for being a doctor was evident in everything he did, from showing her their newest operating room to introducing her to the other doctors and nurses to answering questions. And he didn't make her blood boil in the way Malik did.

Finally, Hassan took her to the ward where she was to paint the mural. She made her way to the middle of the room and slowly turned, taking in the size of each blank, white wall and noting where the windows started and ended.

Murals were always a challenge, but this one much more.

The room would be occupied by children who had enforced stays at the hospital, not of one or two days, but of several weeks or months.

Realizing she'd left her bag in the car, she turned to ask Samir to get it, but he held it out.

"His Highness thought you might need this," Samir said.

"Thank you." She took the bag from his outstretched hand, and then looked at Hassan. "I'd like to spend some time in here alone. Is that okay?"

"Sure. I need to get back to work anyway." Hassan gave her a smile and left.

Catherine moved into the middle of the room once again, before she sat on the floor.

"Shall I get you a chair?" Samir asked.

"No, thanks. But you may want to get one for yourself, I'm going to be here a while." After pulling out her sketchpad, she went to work.

Several hours later, Catherine stood and stretched. Leaning over, she picked up her sketchpad and flipped through the pages. Nothing seemed right. It didn't help that every other sketch was one of Malik. That man had gotten under her skin, and she couldn't figure out how to get rid of him, or if she even wanted to.

This was not good. She needed to concentrate on her job. She glanced at the drawings. While they were good, they didn't fit the room.

If she were going to do this right, she needed to talk to the children who would occupy the room.

Strolling over to Samir, she smiled at him and said, "I need to talk to Hassan."

Samir nodded and pulled out his cell phone. Within minutes, Hassan entered the room. "What can I do for you, Catherine?"

"I'd like to talk with the children who will occupy this room."

Hassan crossed his arms over his chest and stared at her.

"What is it?" She bit her lower lip.

"I'm sorry, Catherine, I'm trying to find a way to put this delicately."

Her fingers tightened on the sketchpad. What was it with this family and dithering? "Just tell me, please."

Placing his hands in the pockets of his white coat, Hassan rocked back on his heels. "Most of the children who will occupy the ward will be long-term-care kids."

"Yes, I've been informed of that." She tilted her head. "I don't understand why you're skirting around this fact. No child should spend his or her days cooped up in a hospital."

"Agreed, but many of the kids have terminal illnesses or have very long recovery times. Many of them will never leave this ward."

Catherine's heart stuttered. No wonder her manager had pushed her to take this job. If anyone understood terminal illness, it was her. Jamie's long, hard-fought battle with cancer had opened her eyes to helping those she could with her art. She'd spent time after Jamie's death with terminally ill children. "I don't have an issue with that." When Hassan didn't answer, she asked, "Is today a bad day? Are there many families visiting?"

"Families are always visiting. It is good for the kids, but … " Hassan spread his hands out in front of him. "Catherine, you do understand that some of these kids have undergone extreme treatments?"

It took a minute, then she realized what he was trying to say. He was afraid she'd react badly to seeing the ill children. "Hassan," she started. "I've spent many days working with terminally ill children at a rehab clinic, trying to brighten their lives with my art. Does that help?"

The relief at her words spilled over his features as he smiled. "Thank you for understanding."

"Let's go see the kids." Catherine concentrated on her breathing as they walked down several hallways to where the current children's ward was.

This was not the time to let her emotions get in the way. But the minute she entered the room, her emotions went into overdrive.

She wanted to gather each child into her arms and promise them they would never hurt again, but realistically that was a promise she couldn't keep. So the best she could do was involve them in the mural and make it come alive for them.

Pasting a smile on her face, she approached the first bed, introduced herself and talked to both the child and family. Slowly, she made her way around the room, talking to each child, until she reached the last one. A nurse sat next to his bed, trying to coax him into eating. The boy stared straight ahead.

Her heart turned over. There was something in his blank stare that brought tears to her eyes. "Who is the little boy?"

she asked Hassan in hushed tones after she walked over to him.

"That's Zain."

"Can you tell me his story? He looks so alone."

"He has no family."

"The poor little guy." Judging by the bandages on his hands, he wasn't able to feed himself. "What happened to his hands?"

"Burns." Hassan let out a sigh. "He was caught in a house fire."

The pain the little boy must have suffered shot through her heart. With a nod to Hassan, she moved over to the bed and pulled up a chair. She gave the nurse a smile, then looked at Zain.

"Hi, Zain, my name is Catherine. Dr. Hassan told me your name, and I thought I'd come and visit you. I've already visited with the other children." She kept her voice low and her tone soothing. "I'm here to paint the mural in the new children's ward, and I wanted to find out what you and the other children want on the walls. How about I show you some drawings and you can tell me which ones you like?"

She lifted her sketchbook and opened it to a page that held an elephant. "Now, what do you think of him?"

❧ 8 ❧

Malik stared in awe as he stopped in the doorway of the children's ward. The sight in front of him caused his heart to swell.

Catherine sat on the floor, Zain in her lap, with the other children sitting around her. Young voices spoke all at once.

But it wasn't the other children that fascinated him, it was Zain. Zain was allowing someone to hold him. Malik closed his eyes with a prayer of thanks. He'd visited Zain every day since the accident, and Zain hadn't reacted to him or anyone else. Just a blank stare. Until today. Until Catherine.

"Let's see." Catherine's voice carried across the room. "What about a jungle background with lions, tigers, zebras, and maybe an elephant or two?"

"Yeah." The chorus of young voices grew loud as they scooted closer to Catherine.

"What else?" she asked, her eyes shining and a smile on her lips. Pride filled Malik. She would make an amazing wife and royal surrogate mother to the ill children. Too bad their engagement was fake.

"A castle," Lyssa, one of the children with cancer, said.

"An amusement park," Cadi said. He had an arm and leg in a cast.

Catherine wrote down each suggestion as the children called them out, then she tilted her head down to Zain. "What do you think, Zain? A castle with an amusement park in the courtyard? What would you like?"

Zain lifted his head until his mouth was close to her ear. To Malik's amazement, the child's lips moved. His Catherine was a miracle worker.

Her face lit up when Zain finished speaking. "What a great idea." She lifted her head. "Zain suggested I include animals from your wonderful country. What do you kids think about that?"

There was another chorus of young voices saying yes, they loved their country. "Very good, children," Catherine said. "I thank you for your help."

"Will we be able to see you paint?" Lyssa asked.

Catherine tilted her head, exposing her neck, and Malik wanted to lower his lips to taste that patch of silky skin. Then he'd run his tongue over her, making her shiver with the same need coursing through him. But not now, not in front of the kids.

"Well, I'll have to ask Dr. Hassan about that." The kids frowned. "It will be a little bit before you'll be able to see anything. The way I work is to first outline the animals, then paint them. That way I don't make a big mistake, like putting elephant ears on a giraffe."

The kids burst out in laughter, but the laughter turned to a groan as a bell rang. Catherine glanced up at one of the adults sitting beyond the circle.

"It's four o'clock. Time for the kids to be back in bed and get ready for dinner," one of the parents told her.

"Okay." Catherine smiled at the children. "Let's get a move on, kids."

Malik watched as the kids scrambled to their feet, some with the help of the adults, and others okay on their own. It was obvious the kids had taken to Catherine, but the adults as well. Words of praise for her and for her including the children in her work floated around the room.

He still stood in the doorway, no one noticing his presence yet, and he wanted to keep it that way. Catherine had set Zain on his feet and then pushed herself up until she was standing. Zain clung to her leg until she picked him up. She was so tender with the child. She would make a great mother.

Malik continued to watch as Zain lay his head on her shoulder as she carried him back to bed. She lay him down on the white sheets, covering him with a blanket, before whispering to him. Not wanting to alert her to his own presence, Malik moved slowly into the room. Catherine was covering Zain with the blanket and brushed a lock of the boy's hair out of his face.

"I'll be back tomorrow, Zain. I have an idea, and I'll have to run it by Dr. Hassan first, but how would you like to be my helper?"

Zain nodded. The boy looked so small under the covers, but Malik was aware he wasn't eating well.

"Good. I'll talk with Dr. Hassan, but you need to be a good boy and eat all your dinner and get a good night's rest." She ruffled Zain's hair, then dropped a kiss on his forehead. "Sweet dreams."

Another miracle appeared. Zain smiled at Catherine. Malik almost pumped his fist in the air and let out a cheer. She'd broken through Zain's protective shell in a single day. He didn't know how she'd done it, but he was happy she had. Convincing her to stay was one of the best decisions he'd ever made.

"Prince Malik?" a soft voice said, catching his attention.

He glanced over at the bed closest to him, where Isis lay with her mother by her side. "Hello, Isis." With a smile, he maneuvered to her bedside.

Catherine's heart caught in her throat as Zain smiled at her. Her goal had been to involve him with the other children, and she was overjoyed he'd responded to her and her sketches. While he would only speak to her in one or two whispered words, it made her heart sing that he did so.

"Until tomorrow, my little friend." She brushed a kiss over his soft cheek before turning to gather her belongings. She jerked when she saw Malik standing across the room.

He was talking to some of the family members as they began filtering out of the room. How long had he been there? She shrugged; it didn't matter. She'd spent all day with the kids and didn't regret one moment of it. Placing the strap of her bag over her shoulder, she moved toward the door.

At the last minute, she glanced back at Zain. He watched her, his eyes glowing, much better than the vacant stare he'd shown when she'd arrived.

"You are a miracle worker," Malik whispered in her ear as he grasped her elbow.

His touch sent shivers of anticipation through her veins. "Nope. I just know how it feels for a kid to feel isolated and alone." While her circumstances had been different than the other kids and Zain, the emotions they experienced were universal.

"I disagree." Malik guided her out of the room to where Samir waited in the hallway. "Zain hasn't responded to anyone since his parents' deaths. He won't let the nurses hold him, yet he allowed you not only to hold him, he cuddled into your embrace, and he smiled at you. That is nothing short of a miracle." His voice was full of pride.

Her heart raced, and while she wanted to attribute it to his words, it was more from Malik's touch, his closeness, than anything else.

"Can you tell me what happened to Zain?" She needed to distract herself from how Malik was making her feel.

"I'll explain on the way home." He guided her down the hallway. "Did you eat today? Samir said you spent most of the day with the children."

Samir glanced over his shoulder and gave her a grin. "Yes. Samir was kind enough to get me some food."

"Good, we can't have the children's favorite artist going hungry." Samir pushed open the glass doors, and they made their way to the waiting car. Catherine was grateful there was no press around.

Once they were seated in the car, she turned to Malik. "So, tell me about Zain."

"It's a tragic story." He relaxed back against the leather, staring at her.

Catherine crossed her arms over her breasts and stared right back at him. "You and Hassan seem to be under the assumption I'm some sort of fragile flower who can't understand trauma. Trust me, I understand." More than she ever wanted to. Part of her wanted to blurt out Jamie's story, but she held back. She wanted to know about Zain, not relive Jamie's death.

Malik nodded. "Zain's father killed his mother."

A gasp escaped her lips. Malik's eyes turned grim. How

bad was this story going to be? Her instincts told her very bad. "Poor kid."

"No one is really sure what happened that night. We do know that Zain's mother was dead before the fire started."

"The fire that caused his burns?"

"Yes." Malik's gaze skittered away, and Catherine closed her hand over his clenched fist. She hated that retelling this story affected him so much. "From what we can determine," he continued, "Zain's father set the fire to cover up his crime, not caring he was about to kill his sleeping son."

"Oh, dear Lord." She could only imagine what Zain had gone through. Her fingernails on her free hand bit into her palm.

"Thankfully, a neighbor saw the flames and was able to pull Zain to safety, but not before he saw his father die."

"Oh, Malik." She tried to stop the rush of tears, but couldn't. They spilled down her cheeks.

"Shh, don't cry." He slid an arm around her and gathered her to him.

Catherine nestled against his chest, pain for Zain filling her. "He's just a baby. How could anyone do that?"

"I don't know." He ran his hands over her back in a soothing motion. "Children are our most precious gift and should be protected."

"Yes, they should be." She sniffled, finally controlling her tears.

"I happened to be in town when this happened. I arrived at the house right after the fire department. Zain was just sitting there staring at the house. I gathered him up and took him to the hospital. He never cried as Hassan tended to his hands." He lifted her chin up and stared into her eyes. "I've made it a point to visit Zain every day, to try and get him to come out of the shell he's built around himself. That's why Zain reacting to you is a miracle in my book."

Catherine basked in the warmth of his gaze. He didn't shy away from her tears like Jamie had. Instead, he embraced her, allowed her to get her emotions out. She lifted her hand and cupped his cheek in her palm. "You are a special man."

Gold flashed in his eyes, his head dipped, and the car stopped. Catherine bit her lip, trying to hide a smile as Malik swore softly. Then a grin curved his lips.

"We'll continue this later," he said, as the door opened.

❧ 9 ❧

Later that evening, Catherine sat in her room, putting the finishing touches on a couple of sketches, when her mobile phone rang.

A smile swept over her lips when she glanced at the caller ID. "Hi, Sara."

"Hey, there, are you busy?"

"No, what's up?" Catherine set her sketchbook aside.

"Well, want to tell me about the pictures popping up in the tabloids of you and a certain crown prince kissing?"

Oh, hell, the paparazzi were busy. Catherine let out a sigh and shook her head. "I can't believe it's already in the tabloids back home."

"Plastered on every front page. Why didn't you tell me there were pictures?"

"I didn't know there were any until they came out." She

shifted in her seat. This was the last thing she wanted, her name in the press. And dang if it didn't prove Malik was right about the paparazzi following her, even if she did go back to Britain.

"I'm sure this will die down," Sara said in a soothing tone.

"Like I believe that one." Catherine rubbed her forehead. It wasn't as if she hadn't known this was a possibility when she'd seen the photos herself, she'd only hoped … what? The press wouldn't go after a big payday? The likelihood of that was a trillion to one.

"Well, let's forget about them. Tell me, how did your first day at the hospital go?"

A grin formed on her lips. "Oh, Sara, it was good, but heartbreaking at the same time. The kids are so cute and friendly. And there is this one little boy, Zain. The poor guy was caught in a fire. He's so adorable."

"Sounds like you're already half in love with Zain."

"I probably am." Catherine laughed. Sara was well aware of Catherine's work with the children's cancer hospital.

"You brighten up the world for these kids. I'm so glad you accepted this job, Catherine."

"I am too." Even with the paparazzi and everything else, seeing the smile on Zain's face today made it worth it.

"Good. Well, I just wanted to check in with you. I've got to get moving and get ready for work."

"Don't let that Dr. Doom get to you," she said, using the nurses' nickname for the doctor they all hated working with.

Sara laughed. "I won't. Talk to you soon."

Catherine hit the end button and set her phone on top of her sketchbook. Her mind wandered back to earlier. After she and Malik had arrived back at the palace, he'd been pulled away by his minister of information. She had gone to her room to get ready for dinner.

Dinner had been quiet, with everyone discussing their day. It was one thing about the royal family that impressed her. A family dinner every night. Not everyone was there all the time, but Anna told Catherine she'd made it a point when the boys were growing up that they all have dinner together and discuss their day.

As her sons had grown into adults, they'd kept the practice up. Tonight, only Malik and Khalid were at the table. Hassan was at the hospital, and Rafi was off somewhere.

A knock on her balcony doors startled her out of her thoughts. She walked over and slid the curtain aside. Malik stood there grinning at her. Catherine unlocked the door, and he pulled it open.

"What are you doing?"

"I promised we'd continue what we started in the car." He pulled the door closed behind him.

"By sneaking in my balcony doors?" Anticipation slithered up her spine.

"This way we won't be disturbed." He glanced around the room. "What have you been working on?"

"Ummm." She backed up and her face grew warm. Damn, she needed to get to her sketchbook. She lunged for it, but Malik was already there lifting it from the table. "No," Catherine protested.

"What is it, little one?" He didn't let go of her sketchpad. "What are you afraid I'll see?"

He flipped the book open.

Catherine groaned and let her hands drop. She backed up a step as he flipped from page to page. Closing her eyes, she reviewed the drawings she'd done. One of Zain, then one of some trees in the garden, then … argh.

Malik had her so wound up, she'd began sketching out various kinky scenes and toys. His deep intake of breath had her opening her eyes. He was staring at her, not her sketchpad. Oh, this wasn't going to be good.

Malik blinked several times, almost not believing what he was seeing. Catherine was kinky. He almost didn't dare to believe it. But, as they say, a picture is worth a thousand words. Hers were worth millions.

He stopped when he saw the drawing of him holding a flogger, standing over a woman tied to a bed. His groin tightened, and he let out a breath before lifting his head.

Their gazes clashed. Wariness shone from her eyes, her shoulders back, as if preparing herself for a blow. "These are quite good," he whispered.

Her eyes widened. "Thank you."

"Let's sit down."

"Let's not." She crossed her arms over her chest. "Those sketches weren't meant for you to see."

He wasn't conveying his feelings right. Since when had it meant so much to him to do so? A long time. Most didn't understand the mental toll it took to be crown prince. Having control in the bedroom allowed him to let go of everything but giving a woman pleasure. It allowed him to be a man and not the crown prince.

Her images stimulated and touched on a truth he kept hidden. Yes, he liked to restrain his lovers, use various toys on them. His lovemaking was never rough or hurtful, just a bit forceful. Catherine hadn't done these drawings for his benefit. He flipped her sketchpad shut and set it back on the table.

"I'm not angry, Catherine. I'm intrigued." There was a spark between them, one he fully intended to explore. Knowing she was interested in kink pushed the spark to a fire. A fire that burned low and hot in his belly.

"What?" Her head tilted to the side.

"Come." He took her hand and drew her over to the small sofa. He sat and then pulled her down beside him, not releasing her wrist.

"Malik," she protested, and started to rise.

"Stay still." He used his deep voice to command her. She stopped and her head snapped up. The surprise in her face almost made him smile. "Tell me, how kinky are you?"

"Should we really be having this conversation?" She tried to tug her arm away.

"Yes." He didn't tighten his hold, but he didn't release her, either. "I'll admit I enjoy restraining my partner." Color flooded her cheeks. "Ah, I see that excites you. So your interest isn't just artistic?"

"Oh, lord, Malik," she whispered.

"Do you enjoy being restrained?" He wasn't going to let her hide. Anticipation flowed through his veins. If she was kinky, they could have so much fun in the bedroom. They were already very compatible from the kisses they had shared; if she enjoyed a little domination in the bedroom, that would be icing on the cake. "Answer me, Catherine."

"Yes, I like it." She shook her head. "This isn't the conversation I pictured having with you." Her shoulders drooped.

"It's one I'm glad we're having." He released her wrist and settled back against the sofa, watching her. "Tell me more."

"There's not much to tell; you saw the pictures."

Yes, he had. His groin tightened, and his dick pressed against the fabric of his trousers. "I saw several beautiful drawings. One of handcuffs, another of a flogger, then a bed with a shadowed figure, and finally a bare-chested man standing over the bed with a flogger."

As he spoke, Catherine squirmed in her seat. Was she excited? He studied her carefully. Yes, her breathing was a bit rapid, her eyes wide, and more than her cheeks were flushed.

"I … " She shook her head.

"I'm not offended." Malik raised his hand and trailed his fingers up her arm, caressing her soft skin.

"If you were, we wouldn't be talking. You would have walked out."

There was a note of bitterness in her voice. Had someone walked out on her because of a little kink? "Tell me, Catherine, do you want to be that woman on the bed in your drawings?"

She took a shaky breath, then said, "Yes."

He grinned. She was being honest with him, and it made him proud. This woman was his match, even if she didn't believe it yet. "Good." He chose his next words carefully. "Have you been in a relationship with kink in the bedroom?"

She shook her head. "I've only read about it."

Malik cupped her chin and raised her face so their gazes met. "While you may find this hard to believe, I'm only dominant in the bedroom." Catherine giggled and he tried to frown at her, but instead he grinned. "Okay, I am outside as well, but that comes with my job."

Her eyes darkened, and Malik cursed himself for bringing up his crown prince status. "I haven't been in a relationship for more than two years now." He wanted her to know that he wasn't going to hold back from her.

"Why do I find that hard to believe?"

Another grin slid over his lips. "Being the crown prince does come with some disadvantages." He wasn't going to lie to her. "There will be scrutiny of our relationship."

"A reason to keep kink in the bedroom."

"Yes." She understood him, which was a plus. "I know this might be hard to understand, but it helps me center myself. To let go of the day's events and concentrate on the one thing I know I'm good at. Pleasing my woman."

"Arrogant much?"

Malik dipped his head until his lips brushed her cheek. "You have no idea."

"I bet I do." She relaxed into his embrace.

"Are you willing to explore with me, Catherine?" Her silence ate at his soul as he cradled her close to him.

"Yes, I am." Her words were soft and quiet.

"Then we will explore together. I will never hurt you and will always stop when you tell me to."

She inhaled and then released her breath. "Thank you."

Malik held her in his arms, just allowing them both time to absorb what they'd talked about, but also because it felt good to have her in his arms.

❦   IO   ❦

Saturday morning, Malik glanced up from the newspaper he was reading as Catherine entered the breakfast room. He folded the paper and set it down.

During the last week they hadn't had much time alone because of his royal duties. He looked forward to escorting her to and from the hospital. However, his minister of information, Omar, had unknowingly delayed the opportunity to explore his passion for Catherine. Each day, Omar insisted on accompanying him to go over state matters while he was waiting for Catherine.

While he could tell Omar their talks could wait, he didn't. His father expected him to be available to any and all of the ministers to discuss Bashir. Luckily, Catherine didn't seem to mind. She wasn't a woman who needed mindless chatter. She was content to sit and watch the scenery on the drive. But he paid close attention to her and her facial expressions.

She listened in on the matters of state his minister relayed to him and his responses. At times she'd smile or display an occasional frown, and sometimes she'd give little shakes of her head. In a way it made him feel better about the job he was doing as crown prince. He enjoyed her input; it meant she was taking their, albeit fake, engagement seriously.

He rose to his feet. "Good morning," he greeted Catherine.

"Sit down." She waved her hand at him, but he waited until she was seated before resuming his.

She poured a cup of coffee, adding cream and sugar before taking a sip. Her eyes closed, and a sigh of bliss left her lips. She'd told him the other day she didn't feel human until she had a cup. Even on the days she was running behind, she had a travel mug filled with coffee.

"So, what is on the agenda for today?" he asked.

"I've arranged for Samir to take me into Bashir City. I want to explore and get a better feeling for Bashir."

"That sounds like a good idea. I should have offered to do that earlier."

She shook her head. "You've been busy, and it's been good for me to spend time at the hospital with the children. I've gotten their ideas; now it's time to soak up the local flavor, so to speak."

"What time are we leaving?"

She stared at him, a frown settling between her eyebrows. "I'm leaving after breakfast."

Malik didn't miss her speaking in the singular, and he hid a smile. If she thought she was going to get away from him that easily, she was sadly mistaken. She buttered two pieces of toast and put some fruit on her plate.

"You'll need more food than that if you're going to be sightseeing all day."

"I'll be fine."

"You don't need to watch your weight, if that's what you're worried about." His gaze raked her from head to toe.

She glared before taking a bite of her toast, then chewed and swallowed. "My figure has nothing to do with it."

"Good. Because I intend to explore your curves, each and every one of them."

Color swept up her neck into her cheeks, but she didn't answer him. Not that he expected an answer; he wanted her as hot and bothered as he was.

"Do you want some eggs or bacon?" he asked, motioning to the covered dishes on the sidebar.

"No, I'm fine with this. I'm not a big breakfast eater. Why are we discussing my eating habits?"

"I want to make sure you have enough energy for our day." He waited to see how she would react.

"Our what?" She dropped her piece of toast and stared at him.

Malik fought grinning. He liked putting her off balance. She was less likely to fight him that way. While she'd turned down the fake engagement, he'd convince her it was the way to go, but first they needed to spend some quality time together. "I'm going to be your escort today." He stood. "I need to go arrange our transportation."

Malik leaned down and whispered in her ear. "We're going to be alone together, and I for one can't wait." He left the room smiling to himself. Today would be fun, he'd see to it.

Catherine stared after Malik. What was he up to? Her skin tingled at his words. To be alone with him? And then there were his words about exploring her body. She wanted to explore his too. They hadn't had much time alone in the last week. Darn it, what was it about him that sent her body into hormonal overload?

But he was a complication she didn't need. He was the crown prince, for heaven's sake. She wasn't made to be under some microscope by the press and by people. She'd had more than enough of that growing up with parents who were a baron and baroness, and she felt that she had never measured up.

Yet all Malik had to do was glance at her or give her one of his sexy bad boy grins, and her body went into overdrive. Thankfully, his minister of information had been a buffer in the car all week. Malik was annoyed with his minister, but it had saved her from her acting on her own desires, which she had no business acting on. Not when she would be leaving in a few months. During the evenings, she had been half expecting him at her balcony doors and then both disappointed and relieved when he'd apparently had late meetings with the king or his ministers that kept him away from her.

And what was he saying about accompanying her today? With a frown, she finished her breakfast. Her thoughts wandered to Malik again. She was getting good at reading him, and that told her she was spending too much time studying him.

Oh, heck, all she had to do was look at her sketchbook. Pages and pages were filled with him. She fought herself on a daily basis, but it didn't seem to be working. She only wanted to get closer to him, to feel his touch and his kiss once again.

With a shake of her head, Catherine drained her coffee cup, picked up her oversized bag, and made her way to the front entrance where she'd told Samir she'd meet him. She came to an abrupt halt upon seeing Malik leaning against the doorjamb.

"Where's Samir?"

Malik straightened. "Getting the car." He pulled open the heavy wooden door and gestured for her to precede him.

Catherine stopped short when Samir pulled up in a silver Jaguar. Whirling around, she tilted her head and looked at Malik. "What is this?" She gestured to the vehicle. She was getting used to the oversized Mercedes or SUV, but this was a powerful sports car.

"Our car for the day."

"*Our* car?" Oh, no. Oh, no. He could not be serious. They were going to be cooped up in that small car together, just the two of them? Malik stood there, arms folded over his chest, staring at her. Oh, crap, he was serious. A tingle of excitement slipped through her blood at the thought of being alone with him in the vehicle.

"Yes." He cupped her elbow, escorting her down the stairs and to the passenger side of the car.

"But ... " Her words trailed off when he placed warm fingers against her lips. Heat exploded in her body, and she barely stopped her tongue from darting out to taste him.

"You want to explore the city, and I'm more than willing to be your guide."

Her heart skipped several beats. "Where are your body-guards?" she mumbled against his fingers. They had to be around somewhere. It was bad enough Samir didn't leave her alone while she was at the hospital. But Malik had so many more, at least three at all times.

"They'll be in a car behind us and staying out of sight. For all intents and purposes, you and I will be alone." He removed his fingers from her lips and opened the car door.

Alone. That was asking for trouble. But instead of protesting, she slid onto the seat and reached for her seat-belt. Where was her sense of self-preservation? It flew away without her thinking about the consequences if the paparazzi caught them together.

Malik slipped behind the wheel and she turned to him.

"Is this really a good idea?" Who was she trying to convince, him or herself?

"It's the best I've ever had." He leaned over. "Besides, it's time for us to learn more about each other and explore this attraction." He dropped a quick kiss on her lips, then put on his seatbelt before starting the car and putting it in gear.

Her lips pulsed from the kiss as he drove away from the palace. She was about to tell him she'd changed her mind when Malik began talking about the history of Bashir. The pride and joy in his tone had her quickly lost in his voice and his world, all thought of sensual things forgotten.

Forty minutes later, they pulled into the parking lot of the zoo. Catherine shook her head. She couldn't believe how fast the drive had passed. Malik's voice had kept her enthralled with his knowledge of history.

He helped her out of the vehicle. "Before you ask, Samir told me about your interest in seeing native animals, so I figured this would be the best place to start our day." He grinned at her. "The early morning hours are the best to visit because the heat is less intense, there are fewer crowds, and the animals are more likely to be out and about."

Unable to help herself, Catherine laughed. Who would think of finding the crown prince at the zoo? "Lead on."

He gave her one of his heart-stopping grins, then tucked her arm through his as they crossed the parking lot to the entrance.

Several employees bowed their heads as they walked

through the gates. Catherine was getting used to seeing people do it. She had asked Malik about it the first day, and he'd explained it was a sign of respect from the people. She stopped when she noticed there weren't any other people around.

"Where is everyone? Are your zoos not a favorite attraction?" She bit her lip when his cheeks turned a dull red.

"The zoo is ours alone, for as long as you want it."

"Ours?" She glanced over her shoulder to see Malik's security detail, headed by Samir, but no one else. "What do you mean? Don't they open soon? Don't tell me they closed down the zoo for your royal visit?"

"We are here before opening hours, and yes, they have closed it." He lowered his head as if he were embarrassed.

"But how fair is that?" She tugged on his arm when he started to walk. "Think about it, Malik. How many families will arrive today to find the zoo closed? How disappointed their children will be because of that."

He frowned. "It is not my choice. Security demands it."

"Oh, posh." She waved her hands in the air. "You're the crown prince. You can do anything you want. There's no danger here, unless I decide to feed you to one of the animals for being so inconsiderate."

"I used this same argument on my minister of information this morning."

"And apparently he won."

"In a way. Since we put out the press release about the mural, we've had more requests to speak with you."

"Me?" Catherine tilted her head and stared at him. "Why would they want to talk to me?"

"Because you are the artist creating it." He leaned closer. "And a beautiful one at that."

Her breath caught in her throat. Every time he said something like that, her bones melted and she wanted to kiss him silly. "Back to the zoo."

Malik grinned. "You are right. The zoo needs to be open to everyone."

"Dang right I am. You have enough security here to protect us." She waved her hand at his full security team of eight.

He let out a laugh and then signaled Samir to his side.

"Sir," Samir said, stopping in front of them.

"Tell them to open the zoo at the normal time."

"But, sir … "

Malik held up his hand. "Don't argue, just do it."

Samir shook his head and stalked off.

When Malik glanced at her she giggled. "He thinks I'm a bad influence on you."

"It doesn't matter what anyone thinks. Your heart is in the right place. Now, shall we get moving before the crowds descend?"

Catherine laughed and danced away. "Lead on, my prince."

Several hours later, Malik scanned for Catherine. He spotted her right where he'd left her five minutes before his going to speak with Samir about their next stop. She was by the oryx enclosure, her pencil flying over the sketchpad. She'd sketched almost every animal in the zoo, even those not native to Bashir, saying she wanted to capture them as they appeared in his country.

Excited, young voices caught his attention. It had been the right decision to open the zoo. Families strolled around, and children exclaimed over the animals. What surprised him the most was the way he was able to blend in. Very few people approached him. Most just smiled and nodded.

There were a few older gentlemen who came up to shake his hand and introduce themselves, but none in a manner his security forces feared.

A set of nervous giggles caused him to turn his head to the right. A group of teenage girls clustered together.

He smiled at one of the girls when she peeked in his direction, only to have her giggle and her face turn red.

"They think you're cute." Catherine's breath brushed over his skin.

"Oh." He hadn't sensed her come up beside him. "Do you think I'm cute?" He couldn't wait to hear her answer.

Her nose wrinkled as she considered the question. "In an autocratic sort of way."

"I'm not autocratic Bossy, maybe."

Catherine snorted. Lord, this woman was so beautiful when she was being herself. Not that she wasn't beautiful all the time, but right now, all her barriers were down. She wasn't worried about anyone seeing her so unguarded, and her inner beauty shone bright like a beacon.

Her eyes sparkled, her cheeks were pink, and her hair was slightly windblown. And he wanted her. More than he'd ever wanted any woman. He'd gone from liking, to lusting, to need in the space of a week. He should be concerned he was in so deep, but he didn't care.

"This from the man who ordered the Arabian Red Fox to show itself."

"You wanted to sketch him. It was the least I could do." He tugged at the collar of his shirt.

She laughed, and his heart turned over at the sound. When had he had so much fun with a woman? A woman who made him think of long hot nights in his bed, yet at the same time made him so happy? This was the woman he wanted in his life.

"Sir," Samir said.

Catherine stiffened and her smile faded. She backed away from him. All morning that had happened. Each time he and Catherine seemed to get close to each other, one of his security team had interrupted.

"Yes, Samir." Malik tried to keep the irritation out of his voice.

Samir glanced at Catherine, then back at Malik.

"I'll be right over there." She motioned to the empty space near the teenage girls.

"Now what?" This time he didn't hide his annoyance.

"I'm sorry, sir, but the minister of information is on the phone again." Samir held out the small cell phone.

Malik snatched the device out of Samir's hand, barely resisting the urge to smash it to small pieces. "Enough! Whatever it is can wait until tomorrow. Do not call again." He hit the end button and handed the phone back to Samir. "Unless it's a member of my family, do not answer it." Without another word, he strode to Catherine.

"Do we need to get back?" she asked, not looking at him but rather at the foliage.

"No." He combed his fingers through his hair before dropping them back to his side.

"If you need to go back, I'm okay with it." She placed a soft hand on his forearm, and every nerve in his body went on alert.

The urge to snatch her into his arms and kiss her was strong. Her offer was sincere, and it was precious to him. "We're fine."

He took her hand and brought it to his mouth. His lips caressed her knuckles. A fine shiver ran up her arm.

He wanted, no needed, to kiss her. Now. A chorus of feminine sighs floated on the air. They had an audience; maybe that would work to his advantage. He released her hand and framed her waist.

"Malik, what are you doing?" she whispered.

"I'm going to kiss you." He slid his body closer to hers.

"Why?" She tilted her head, looking up at him.

"Because I want to." He captured her lips with his.

Ambrosia. She tasted of sweetness and pleasure. He had planned on making it a short kiss, but she let out a sigh, and her lips opened to his as she leaned into him.

He couldn't help himself; he allowed his tongue to slip past her lips, tangling with hers, playing with it, before exploring the deep recesses of her mouth. Her arms encircled his neck, causing his skin to tingle, then she dug her fingers into his hair. He widened his stance, pulling her between his legs, letting her feel what she did to him.

For a brief moment, she stiffened, then she pressed even closer as her tongue traced his. Malik bit back a groan. How long would it take them to get back to the palace and his bed?

A series of feminine sighs caused Catherine to break the kiss. She glanced over her shoulder, and Malik followed her gaze. The girls were staring at them with awe etched in their expressions.

"I think you made their day," she whispered, wishing her heart would stop pounding. Heck, who was she kidding, her core was pulsing with want and need. If they'd been alone … but they weren't.

"It made mine." He brushed his thumb over her lower lip. "I want to keep kissing you. I want to make love to you with my lips, to hear you sigh my name as you orgasm. Shall we return to the palace?"

A hyena let out a bay, and Catherine's heart sank. What was wrong with her? Anyone could snap a picture. But to return to the palace? It took her brain several seconds to catch up with her emotional high.

He was aroused, and darn it, so was she. But to sleep with him? Bad idea. Kissing him hadn't been such a good idea either, but she'd been unable to help herself.

Determined to put some space between them, she tried to take a step back. He held her fast.

"No hiding, Catherine."

"What are you talking about?" She squirmed in his hold. A minute ago she couldn't wait to be closer to him; now, she needed distance between them or she might do something stupid, like beg him to tie her up and have his wicked way with her.

"I mean, my fair princess, this is only the beginning. You can't hide from me or your destiny."

"Want to bet?" Her stomach chose that moment to let out a growl.

Malik threw back his head and laughed, allowing some precious space between their bodies.

"Later, when we are alone, we will explore this," he whispered. "Right now, I think a snack is in order, then a visit to the marketplace." He stepped away from her but captured her hand, and they walked toward the zoo entrance.

"This is magnificent," Catherine said a short time later as they strolled around town. The wrought-iron balconies reminded her of the intricate ironwork in the French Quarter of New Orleans. Then there were the latticework shutters, which protected the occupants from the harsh sun and the occasional sandstorms. At least that's what Malik told her. But it was the marketplace that held her captivated. Rows upon rows of every conceivable type of merchandise made it a shopper's paradise.

Choices ranged from fruits and vegetables, to spices, to shoes, to the latest Paris fashions, to more traditional Bashir clothing, to furniture, to the most up-to-date electronic equipment. Her senses were overwhelmed, yet a thread of excitement ran through her veins. This was a tour of a lifetime. Vendors, each one friendly, called out greetings as she and Malik walked down the narrow streets.

Many recognized Malik. They smiled and invited him to view, taste, or simply see what they were selling. And word of his presence passed through the marketplace, because as they walked, more and more people filled the streets.

Malik was gracious, stopping and talking to the vendors. Catherine stood back and observed, then pulled out her small digital camera. She couldn't resist taking pictures of Malik surrounded by his people.

The people were very respectful, but they were also very anxious to talk with him. From her vantage point, she watched as he took each person's hand or touched a child on the head and, in some cases, embraced an elderly woman. And he listened to each person. He was very much a public official. He was truly the people's prince.

And she had no idea of how to deal with him. He was a public figure, more so than Jamie ever had been. And Malik made her heart pound and her core clench with need. A small shiver of fear climbed up her spine. She could lose herself to this man if she wasn't careful.

"Your people respect and love you," she commented after Malik rejoined her and they were seated at a table in a local cafe.

"And that is a bad thing?" He snagged her fingers and raised them to his lips.

"No." A shiver trailed from the tips of her fingers to her toes. Part of her enjoyed the attention Malik lavished on her, while yet another part was overwhelmed. She hadn't been the focus of male attention in quite a while.

She should be distancing herself from him. Not allowing him to kiss her fingers, to overwhelm her senses. In the long run it could hurt them both. Tomorrow, she promised. She wanted to enjoy today, these moments in his country and his company.

"You're a good man and an even better royal. It's obvious that in everything you do, you do it for your people and your country."

A frown appeared. He gazed at her, and she wondered if she'd stepped over an imaginary boundary.

"You are very observant."

"It comes with being an artist." She shrugged and picked up the menu in front of her. The words jumbled together because all she could concentrate on was him.

She opened her mouth to ask him what he would suggest when a camera flash went off.

❦ 12 ❧

Catherine flinched and hid behind the menu.

"Prince Malik, Miss Taylor, look this way," one of the reporters said.

"You've been to the zoo and now the marketplace. Why such an eclectic tour?" yelled another.

Malik swore. Catherine wished a sandstorm would swallow her. This was the last thing she wanted. She didn't need the press around her.

"Miss Taylor, how do your parents feel about your being with the crown prince?" The question was yelled, even as Malik's bodyguards pushed the paparazzi back.

Her hands began to shake. Oh, no, this couldn't be happening. Catherine closed her eyes and tried to find the calm place within, but it wasn't there. Thoughts jumbled around in her brain, along with fear and dread.

She fought against the urge to run and bit her lower lip, trying to find a way to control her emotions. Everything had been fine until she came to Bashir and met Malik. The press had left her alone for more than a year now. Why hadn't she left when she'd found out who he was?

Because she was a professional, and she had a job to do. She wouldn't let the children down, let alone her manager. But her mental well-being was on the line.

"Catherine?" Malik said, concern lacing his tone.

She ignored him and found the small, safe place inside her mind. There, nothing could hurt or touch her. She lowered the menu and looked at him. "I'd like to go back to the palace now." Her voice was devoid of all emotion as she stood.

Malik followed suit, signaling Samir. But when he tried to take her arm, she shied away. No, she couldn't handle him touching her right now, because she'd sink into his warm and tender care. She refused to give the press more fodder.

The paparazzi were still shouting questions and snapping pictures when she and Malik climbed into the car Samir had brought around.

"Catherine," Malik started as the vehicle drove away from the press.

"No." She put a hand up to stop his words. "I can't talk right now." Catherine scooted to the far side of the seat and stared out the window without seeing anything. She kept her face blank and her hands clasped together in her lap as they returned to the palace.

Once they arrived, she barely waited for her door to be opened and quickly made her way inside and up to her room. Unable to settle down, she paced the living room area. The day that had started out with so much promise was now a disaster. Well, almost. She'd discovered Malik was a tender, caring man, and darn if her heart didn't stutter each time she was with him.

It had to stop. She was here to do a job.

Striding over to the French doors, she opened them and stepped out onto the balcony. Her heart might want Malik, but her mind couldn't handle the chaos that came with him. Were the paparazzi already making connections? They'd asked her about her parents. A simple question, but one she knew wouldn't stay that way once they started digging. It wouldn't take much more time before they connected other dots.

Once they latched onto a story, they'd keep digging, and they'd find out about Jamie. She didn't want to relive her horrid childhood with her parents nor Jamie's death. She didn't want to see the sympathy in Malik's eyes or have him feel the need to defend her.

She'd done nothing wrong except lose her temper. She needed to get her emotional wall back up. That's all there was to it. Wall up, Malik out. She couldn't risk letting Malik behind that wall again. Nope, it was time to fortify it with stronger stones.

Catherine squeezed her eyes shut. But she didn't want to shut him out. That was part of the problem. She wanted to see where this attraction for him went. With a shake of her head, she marched back inside her room. Concentrate on your work and nothing else, she told herself. Grabbing her bag, she pulled out her sketchpad and dumped the rest of the contents on the desk. The sooner she finished the job, the sooner she could leave with her heart and soul intact.

Malik cursed under his breath, not only for the paparazzi and their intrusion, but because they'd pushed Catherine back into her shell. He and Catherine had had a perfect day until that point. Who had tipped the press off?

Oh, it wasn't unusual for the press to follow him around during official functions, but today had been anything but official, and only those close to him had known about the outing.

Yes, someone at the zoo or marketplace could have called the press as well, but it seemed unlikely. The people would not have told the press where he was; they were forever shooing them off when they followed him. It had to be someone who knew his habits. He always went to Belim's for coffee and a snack when he was in town. Maybe someone from there or maybe someone from inside the palace.

His brothers and parents wouldn't have said anything. It was possible a servant could have accidentally let something slip. Malik clenched his hands. Damn paparazzi. He turned and strode down the hallway to his father's office. His father was sitting at his desk.

"Who else knew I was taking Catherine out today?" Malik asked the instant he walked into the office.

His father's head snapped up. "What happened?"

"Paparazzi."

"You knew this was a possibility."

"Not today." Malik paced around his father's office. "Only the family and security were aware of this trip. I want to know who tipped them off." He was shouting, but he didn't care. Someone had hurt Catherine, and he wanted their head for it.

"Malik, calm down."

"How can I?" He glared at his parent. His father hadn't seen Catherine retreat inside herself once again. "Catherine is upset, her day ruined by the paparazzi, and I'm positive she'll be in her room for the rest of the day."

"And you, son, need to clear your head of emotions and start thinking logically. Who has the most to gain by exposing her to the press?" His father's voice was calm.

Malik took a deep breath, then let it out. His father was right. His emotions were tying him up in knots. Flopping onto a chair, he stared at his father. "I have no idea."

"Then let us discuss it. Tell me about your day."

For two hours they went over every detail of the day, and nothing stood out. Neither one of them could find an answer. When Omar strode into the room, Malik barely bit back a groan.

"What is it now?" He'd had enough of this man for the day.

"Tomorrow's papers." Omar set them on Malik's father's desk. "You will not like them."

Malik picked up the first paper and read the headline. "Royal Artist Betrayed Her Family." What the hell?

He started reading the article. "The parents of Catherine Taylor, a British citizen, have come forward explaining that their daughter has forsaken them because she doesn't share their values. They have also expressed their daughter may have some mental issues stemming from the death of her lover, singer Jamie Monroe."

Malik threw the paper down and picked up the next one, and then the next. All of them were along the same theme. That wasn't Catherine at all. What kind of crap were these people shoveling to a willing press? He looked his father in the eye. "What's the plan?"

"We don't have much of a choice. We replace this story with a bigger one. We announce your engagement to Catherine."

"She hasn't agreed to it." Malik rubbed his forehead; he didn't like this at all.

"The crown prince is correct, Your Majesty. Ms. Taylor doesn't seem to like the idea of an engagement, even a fake one," Omar said.

"I know, but we don't have a choice in the matter now. We have to stop the rumors, the innuendo. Catherine shouldn't suffer because the paparazzi can't tell a real story from a fake."

"So, basically, damage control," Malik said, not liking the idea of doing this without Catherine's permission, but she'd been upset and right now he didn't want to upset her more. But his father was right, if they didn't nip this in the bud, it would grow even bigger. Give the press a bigger story, and they'd forget this one. At least they could control the narrative over the engagement.

"Yes. Let's get this drafted up," the king said.

"Your Majesty, I strongly object," Omar said.

"Noted, but this will be done by my orders. No more arguments."

Malik nodded. Catherine might be upset with them, but it was the only way to protect her now. And he would protect her the best he could. "Let's get this done."

❧ 13 ❦

The next morning, Catherine glanced up at the hospital walls. Outlines barely visible to the naked eye now graced the blank walls. Raising her arms above her head, she tried to stretch the kinks out.

She'd left the palace yesterday—okay, left wasn't the right word—she'd snuck out. Years of experience had taught her how to get past bodyguards and escape. She'd found a weakness in the garden and used it to her advantage. Once free, she'd taken her time and walked to the hospital. It really wasn't that far from the palace, and the exercise had done her some good.

She'd spent most of the night working on the mural, catching a few hours' sleep early this morning before resuming her work. Now she had a sense of peace within her, as she always did when she worked. Pausing, she looked over at Zain, who sat in the middle of the floor watching her.

"What do you think, Zain?" He'd been with her all morning, never saying a word but staying close to her.

And while Zain had slipped behind her protective wall, that was okay. He was a child, and he couldn't hurt her. Not like Malik could.

"Yeah, I know," she continued as if Zain had answered her. "It doesn't look like much now, but tomorrow I'll start painting, and then it will take shape."

"Only if you're still alive," a familiar male voice whispered in her ear.

Catherine's heart stopped beating, and when it restarted, it pounded in triple time. She angled her head, staring into Malik's dark eyes.

A flame of anger and … passion flared within them.

"Hi," she said, starting to move away from him, but he captured her by the shoulders and held her in place.

"You're not going anywhere." He smiled at Zain. "Hey, Zain. Hassan is going to take you back to your room. I need to talk with Catherine."

Zain nodded, and Catherine watched as Hassan led the little boy out of the room. Then she noticed Malik's two other brothers were there, along with most of his security staff.

"We'll give you some privacy," Rafi said, nudging Khalid before they all filed out.

The air vibrated in the silence. Catherine's muscles

screamed at being held so rigidly, but she wasn't about to move. She didn't want to disturb the sleeping tiger that was Malik, because she had a feeling he was ready to pounce the second she did.

"Would it help if I said I'm sorry?" She forced herself to breathe naturally.

"For what?" Malik stared at her. His eyes were still blazing, but his hold on her shoulders relaxed slightly.

"For whatever has you so upset."

"What has me upset?" Malik shook his head. "I really want to shake some sense into you, but I'm so relieved at finding you safe my anger is draining away."

"Of course I'm safe."

Malik took a deep breath, inhaling her unique scent. "Do you know you have the entire household in an uproar?" He slid his hands from her shoulders and down her arms to her waist. Slipping them around her, he secured her close to him. If he had it his way, she'd be in his arms from now on, where he could be sure she was safe.

"Why?" She twisted her head back and stared up at him.

"Why? After you went upstairs yesterday, I didn't expect to see you for the rest of the day, but this morning when you didn't show up for breakfast, we all became concerned. Imagine my mother's surprise and fear when she went to your room, and not only found it empty, but your bed hadn't been slept in, and the balcony doors were wide open."

"I left the balcony doors open?" She didn't remember

shutting them, so it was possible. Catherine squirmed in his embrace, but he wasn't releasing her. "I couldn't settle down and figured I'd work on the mural. I did leave a note," she said.

"Yes, but it took myself and Khalid to find it. And a note that just said, "Don't worry." Did you not think to call when you got to the hospital, or something?"

"I'm sorry." Her voice was soft.

"Samir is blaming himself."

"It's not his fault." She bit her lower lip.

"Security is tight, and later you will tell us how you managed to get past them, because it never should have happened." Malik lowered his head until his lips brushed against her ear. "Even with the note. We didn't know if you'd been kidnapped or something worse. Not only is my security team on alert, but the entire security force of the city. Thankfully, one of the nurses thought to call Hassan a little while ago when she saw you without Samir."

"Again, I'm sorry. I didn't mean to cause anyone to worry about me. That was never my intention." She strained away from him, but Malik wasn't about to let her escape. Not now. Not ever. He'd made his decision in the frantic hours of that morning when trying to find her. Part of his heart had been ripped away at the thought of something happening to her.

He closed his eyes and inhaled. The scent of honey invaded his senses. Turning her in his embrace, he gazed down at her.

"I know it wasn't your intention, but we were worried. Why did you come to the hospital?"

"I wanted to lose myself in my work." Her gaze skidded away from his. She wasn't telling him the full story.

"And not face the paparazzi or my family?" She ducked her head. "I don't blame you, but by running away, you've made things worse." Her head snapped up, his words finally getting her full attention.

"How?"

"I will explain when we get back to the palace."

"Explain now."

The stubborn look on her face told him she wouldn't budge until he told her. "Rafi," he called out.

No matter what his brothers had said about leaving them alone, they'd stay within shouting range. Catherine's disappearance had jolted all of them out of their comfort zones. Maybe they needed to be jolted, as they'd become a little too complacent. Including security. Khalid was not happy.

"What do you need?" Rafi stuck his head inside the door.

"Would you please bring me the morning papers?"

Rafi nodded and disappeared.

Malik didn't want to let Catherine go, but in order for her to see what her running had done, he would have to. He removed his arms from around her waist as his brother brought several folded newspapers to him.

"Thank you."

"Sure." Rafi glanced at Catherine. "Don't be too hard on him," he said before walking back to stand by the door.

"What is he talking about?" She had taken a couple of steps back.

"We had a plan in place, and we were prepared to discuss it with you, but your leaving made us switch to plan B."

"Why did you need a plan?"

Malik held his tongue and instead opened the first paper. He handed it to her and waited for the explosion.

Catherine took the paper. He watched her face as she read the headline. He already knew what it said. She hadn't given him a choice.

❧ 14 ❧

"The king and queen have announced Crown Prince Malik's engagement to Miss Catherine Taylor. The engagement party will be held at a later date."

Catherine took a deep breath after reading the headline. What the hell?

"Surprise," Malik said.

"Surprise?" Catherine choked back hysterical laughter. "How about untrue, unfounded, totally ridiculous, and downright crazy?"

Laughter erupted. From the doorway, Rafi said, "She's not going to be a pushover, brother."

"I never thought she would be."

Catherine swallowed hard as Malik took the paper from her shaking hands and took one of her hands in his. "I can explain what is happening."

She thought about refusing, but as she stared at Malik, there were fine lines of strain around his eyes and mouth. Her anger at the press headlines drained out of her. Hell, the press was always making stuff up. She couldn't blame Malik for what they did. She had to shoulder some of the blame. She was the one who had run off and put the royal household in an uproar. But why this announcement? Was this a typical paparazzi game or a game on Malik's part?

"Okay, explain."

With a nod, he turned to the door. "Out," he said to Rafi, who scrambled out the doorway. Malik turned back to face her.

"It wasn't easy for me to make the announcement." He squeezed her fingers, his dark eyes brewing a minor storm.

"Why did you make it at all? The press had enough to make up crap on their own, why feed them this lie?"

He sighed and released her hand. "For several reasons." He slid another set of newspapers from under his arm and handed them to her. "What you are seeing here is what the headlines would have been if I hadn't made the announcement."

Catherine glanced at the first paper and swayed.

Front and center was a picture of her parents, with the headline, "Our Daughter Has Betrayed Us." She closed her eyes, praying for strength, then opened them and flipped to the next paper. The headline screamed, "Is Prince Malik Unfit to Be King?" while the first lines of the article read,

"Tribal leaders concerned about his relationship with artist."

"I'm sorry," she whispered. She didn't need to read any more. This was bad, very bad. She was destroying Malik's reputation and that of his family. And her parents? Attention-seeking, narcissistic idiots. The warmth of Malik's hands covering hers caused her to raise her gaze to his. Instead of the disgust she expected to see, there was only concern.

"You have nothing to be sorry for. Well, except for running." He leaned closer to her. "Kalif, one of the tribal leaders, has been trying for years to overthrow my father. He saw you as the way to try and convince people I am not worthy to take over my father's position when he decides to step down."

"But you are," she burst out. In the short time she'd been there, she'd watched the way he took his responsibilities seriously. He was always working. While she was at the hospital, he would take calls or talk with his ministers. She'd watched him in action with his people; they would seek out his counsel or ask him for help. It didn't matter how tired he was, he would always talk with them. Even at the hospital, the staff had nothing but praise for him and his family.

"Thank you." He inclined his head. "It's nice to know you feel that way."

"I'm sure most of Bashir does. Why does this Kalif want to discredit you?"

"It's a long story. I made the announcement of our

engagement not only because of Kalif, but because of what the press is digging up on you."

She shook her head. What was he thinking about her? What did his family think? Did she even want to know?

"I promised to protect you from them," he continued. "I've done a poor job of it."

"They were bound to figure it out sooner or later." And what else would they dig up? She didn't think her parents would talk about Jamie, but the barn door was open. She let out a sigh.

"You've never mentioned your parents." His voice was soft and soothing.

"No. It's not a pretty story." Lord, would he think of her as a poor little rich girl? She couldn't help the circumstances of her birth. Her parents were royalty. On the very lowest branch of the chain, but they were still there. They spent money as fast as it came in, but attended every royal function they could to get in front of the press, and until Catherine left, they had made her attend as well, no matter how much she'd hated it.

"I suspected from that piece." He gestured toward the papers still in her hand.

"You read it?"

He nodded. Catherine squeezed her eyes shut. This was worse than she'd thought. Fear slipped its icy fingers through her veins.

"You have nothing to be ashamed of," he said, his voice close to her ear. "You are your own woman. Your choices are your choices. I've made some less than favorable ones over the years, but that is a part of life."

"And the engagement?" Why such an extreme announcement? She'd only been in the country a little over a week. People were not going to believe this nonsense.

"That, I ask you to go along with." His voice was resigned. "I was going to discuss it with you this morning, but then we found you were gone."

Catherine sighed. Old feelings surfaced about the press and their impact on her life. Catherine tried to fight them. "You're using me." Like her parents and Jamie had.

"No." He shook his head, his lips pressed into a thin line.

"Yes," she countered. "Just like you did at the airport. You're trying to divert attention from the real issues."

His body recoiled from her direct hit. Malik opened his mouth, then closed it. His jaw clenched. "Partially." He grasped her by the shoulders and stared into her eyes. "Yes, I'm trying to divert attention from the issues your family is bringing up to the press. I'm trying to shield you as much as I can."

"And Kalif?" Part of her melted at his wanting to protect her, but the other part just wanted a man who would ignore her family and her past and love her for just being herself.

"I can't afford to allow Kalif to sway the other tribe members. I'm asking you, please, allow our engagement announcement to stand until I can gain an agreement with the other tribal leaders."

Catherine hated this out-of-control feeling invading her life. It had happened with her parents and then with Jamie; now it was happening with Malik. She just wanted a nice quiet life. The kiss at the airport she could deal with, the press following them around was harder, but to become engaged? This was a life-changing event, even more so because of Malik's position as crown prince.

And just how temporary would this engagement be? While she was here working? Or longer? "I need to think about this." But what was there to think about? It was a done deal.

Malik inclined his head, and defeat crossed his features before he wiped it away. "Shall we go back to the palace?"

"Yes." Catherine shoved the newspapers into Malik's hands before gathering up her materials. When they left the room, not only did Malik's bodyguards surround them, but so did Rafi, Hassan, and Khalid. "Is this necessary?"

"Unfortunately, yes." Malik cupped her elbow. "Prepare yourself, this will not be pleasant. There is a massive amount of press outside."

Several of the guards pushed open the doors. The noise of the crowd waiting hit Catherine like an unexpected sandstorm. Oh, dear Lord, questions began flying along with camera flashes.

Malik curved his arm around her shoulders, anchoring her to his side as his guards pushed through the crowds. His brother held a jacket over their heads as they made their way to the waiting vehicle.

Catherine was grateful for their help, along with Malik's protection. At least this time she wasn't alone. And the impact of what was happening smacked her. What if Malik hadn't found her? If she'd walked out of the hospital unprotected? A shiver ran up her spine. She trembled.

"A few more feet," Malik whispered, his lips brushing her ear.

She nodded, and within a minute she was in the vehicle and the door slammed shut, cutting the noise level. The car moved slowly until they were free of the crowd.

The drive was silent, but Catherine was aware of people on the street pointing at the car as they drove by. She couldn't miss the press camped out at the palace gates. The second the car stopped, she turned to Malik. "I'm so sorry," she said before opening the door and fleeing.

Minutes later, she was in the middle of the garden, trying to catch her breath. Thoughts chased each other around her brain until they became muddled. Finding a bench beneath the shade of a large palm tree, she sat and thought about what she should do. She started to catalogue everything that had happened since she'd arrived in

Bashir.

Malik's kiss in the airport taking her breath away, the ride to the palace, meeting the king and queen, Malik in the garden, and finding out he was the crown prince. Then there was their exchange on the balcony. Malik at the hospital with her and the kids. Zain. Her heart squeezed. Their morning at the zoo and then the marketplace before the press interrupted.

She argued with herself that she was getting in too deep, and there was only one solution. She would leave, to protect Malik and his family. It wouldn't be easy for her, as it meant leaving the mural undone, but circumstances dictated it. A small voice reminded her that she was running away from her problems. Yes, but this time the stakes were too high; they involved the royal family and her heart.

Maybe in a few months, when things calmed down, she could return and finish the mural. Lord, she hated to leave, it was unprofessional. The kids would be so disappointed, and what about Zain? Her stomach clenched. Her choices were so limited, and this was about self-preservation. She'd pack and ask Samir to take her to the airport. It wouldn't matter if the paparazzi followed, once she was past the security gates, they couldn't touch her, at least not until she landed at Heathrow.

Malik could come up with another headline to distract the press, he was so good at it. With that plan in mind, she jogged up the stairs to her room and pulled out her suitcase.

"You can't leave."

Catherine gave a small scream and spun around. Malik sat lounging on one of the sofas, his dark hair standing out against his white shirt and pants. His gaze was piercing, yet so relaxed, as if he were a modern-day sheik waiting for his latest woman to be brought to him.

Trying to calm her pounding heart, she lashed out at him. "You idiot, you scared me."

"I apologize for scaring you." He rose and the room shrunk. His tall, lean, powerful body called to her as he prowled the floor, closing the distance between them.

"I accept your apology. Now, if you'll excuse me, I have some packing to do."

"You're not going anywhere."

"What?" Catherine stared at him. This wasn't the easygoing Malik she was used to; his tone was flat, yet authoritative. A tone he hadn't taken with her before now. Her muscles stiffened. She wasn't one of his staff required to take his orders.

"You can't leave, Catherine. I won't allow it."

"You won't *allow*?" Words almost failed her. She was overcome with anger at his words and his tone. "Don't you dare tell me what I'm allowed to do. I'm a free person, and I will leave if I want to."

"Without finishing your job?"

His words scored a direct hit to her heart. She'd never left a job undone before, and the kids had been so excited. "You're not giving me a choice."

"I've done what I've had to do, not only to protect my country, but to protect you as well." Malik prowled around the room.

"And I'm doing what I have to do." She crossed her arms over her chest.

"The children will be disappointed, especially Zain."

Her stomach contracted as if he'd physically hit her. She'd grown close to the little boy, and she didn't want to leave him. "That's not fair."

"I'll use everything in my arsenal." He stopped in front of her and grasped her shoulders. "I know this is the last thing you want, but I really had no choice. If I don't take the focus off what everyone is speculating about, I can't accomplish my duties, and neither can you."

"I understand that, but you need to understand using me as a deflection won't work. It never has."

"It will if you allow it."

She shook her head. It hadn't worked with Jamie. "No, Malik." She placed her hands against his chest.

"Yes. We're good for each other," he whispered as he lowered his head.

His mouth was warm against hers. His lips dominated hers, his tongue tracking the seam of her lips, coaxing her into opening for him. And damn it, she did. Her body betrayed her as her bones melted until she leaned into his embrace. She entwined her arms around his neck, digging her fingers into his hair.

It was so unfair his dominance turned her on, but she couldn't resist him, and honestly she didn't want to. It had been too long since she'd been in the arms of a man who aroused her, who made her feel special.

"No." The word escaped as she tore her mouth from his. She couldn't do this; she couldn't afford to fall under his spell. Disengaging her arms from around his neck, she pushed against his shoulders and was able to put some space between them. She lifted her chin and looked him in the eye. "Kissing me isn't going to get you your way." But damn, it almost had.

His dark gaze hardened. "What will? Jewels? Money? A promise you'll never have to work another day as long as you live?"

She fell back several steps as if he'd slapped her. "Is that what you really think this is about? That I want something from you?" How could he misjudge her that way? She hated the way her parents had used her to get what they wanted, and she would never do that to another person.

"Then tell me, what do you want from me?" He threw his hands in the air. Frustration simmered in the room and in his expression. "Most women would jump at the chance to be with me, yet you treat me like I have the plague. You refuse to let me protect you, to make sure you're safe."

"I'm not like other women," she whispered.

"So I'm finding out." He paced around her room. "I cannot undo what I've done. You'll have to find a way to cope with it." With that, he marched out of the room.

Catherine sank down onto the sofa and let her head drop onto her palms. Her world was going crazy, and she had no idea what she was going to do.

She snatched her cell off the table where she'd left it the day before. There were several missed calls and texts from an unknown number—she guessed those were from Malik —and several more from Sara.

Damn. She opened Sara's messages and scrolled through them.

Saw the papers. Call me!

I'm worried about you.

Call me back.

You're not answering. Where are you? Catherine, answer me.

Catherine looked at the time. It was mid-afternoon. Sara would be at work. Catherine hit reply and typed: *Sorry, Sara, things got a little out of control. I'm all right.*

Within a minute her phone rang with an incoming call. "I really am sorry I worried you, Sara."

"I'm just glad you're okay. I've only got a few minutes. What the heck is going on?"

Catherine quickly explained what had happened and why she'd been out of touch.

"Crap, I've got to go, but you need to get to the bottom of what is going on and your involvement in it. Promise me not to forget your phone again."

"I promise. Thanks, Sara." The phone went silent, and Catherine just stared at it.

Sara was right, she needed answers, and Malik didn't seem inclined to help her, but then again, she hadn't really given him a chance. His scent lingered in the room, and a shiver went up her spine. Escape was all she could think of. With quick movements, she stood and left her room. She knew one person who might answer her questions, someone who would know the whole story of why the engagement was necessary.

Within a couple of minutes, Catherine stood outside King Jamal's office. She knocked and heard a quiet, "Come in," then thanked her escort and entered the king's office. She was surprised there were no guards outside his office.

"Catherine, this is a surprise," Jamal said, making an effort to rise.

Something was very wrong. Rushing to his side, she pushed him back into his chair. His face was pale.

"Jamal," she said, softly touching his forehead and arm. His skin was clammy and his breathing labored.

"I'm so sorry for this press mess, my dear." He held out a hand.

She took it and squeezed. "Shhh, don't worry." She grabbed the phone with her free hand, cradled the receiver, and punched one zero. She was pretty sure Jamal was having a heart attack.

Had she caused this? Had the press been too much even for Jamal? Oh, dear lord. When the phone was answered, she gave security the information and hung up. Catherine waited. Where were they?

"Easy, Jamal. Concentrate on breathing in and out, don't worry about anything else." She glanced at the door, which stayed stubbornly closed.

"You're perfect for Malik." Jamal's voice was soft.

"We'll make it work." The door opened and within minutes, organized chaos descended.

Hassan rushed to his father's side, listening to his heart. Catherine tried to release Jamal's hand, but he held fast. It wasn't until the paramedics arrived, and Hassan gently pried Jamal's fingers loose, that Catherine left her post.

Anna stood in the doorway, her face frozen in terror, and tears spilled down her cheeks. Rafi, Khalid, and Malik stood next to her, their faces lined with worry and concern.

Without thought, Catherine pulled Anna into her arms. "It will be okay," she whispered. Her gaze met Malik's, and she reached out and ran her fingers over his cheeks. "He's a strong man," she continued, more to Malik than his mother. Malik leaned into her touch, as if receiving comfort from her contact. He pulled away as another set of paramedics arrived with a gurney. Then the king was loaded onto the gurney and wheeled out to the ambulance.

"You must come with us," Anna said, gripping Catherine's hand.

"Of course," she said, worried and concerned for everyone.

An entourage of cars arrived and Catherine stayed with Anna as Anna's sons took a different car. Once at the hospital, Catherine barely noticed the reporters or anyone else, for that matter, as she kept close to Anna. Anna needed her support. But Malik was there, supporting his mother as well.

Once inside the waiting room, she guided Anna over to one of the plush sofas and made sure she sat down. When Catherine turned, Malik was there. Lines of worry grooved his face.

She took his hand and gave it a squeeze. "He's a strong man. He'll be okay." She was repeating her words, but it was all she could think of at the moment.

"He has to be." Malik's voice was husky with emotion.

Catherine's heart stopped. Even as powerful as Malik was, he needed his father's strength. No man should have to lose his father so young. She glanced around the room. Rafi and Khalid paced near the windows. Samir and three other bodyguards stood near the doors, their faces grim. Hassan was nowhere to be seen—he was probably at his father's side.

Her stomach clenched. Jamal was important to each person in that room in a different way. She drew Malik into her arms and held him close. "I'm here and I'm not going anywhere." She wouldn't let him go through this alone, not like she'd had to do with Jamie. She'd deal with the fake engagement to protect them.

Malik pushed the remains of his food away as they sat in the hospital waiting room. His mind replayed the events of the past twelve hours. How long before they knew something concrete? Hassan had come out briefly to tell them their father was doing well, but then disappeared again. His gaze searched the room and landed on Catherine, his angel in all this chaos. Even while he and his brothers took turns pacing the private waiting room, she kept everyone calm. Arranging for coffee and food to be brought, sitting next to his mother, coaxing her into eating something, then to lie down on the small cot and rest. She bullied him and his brothers into eating and drinking as well. She even made sure Samir and the other guards ate. Admiration filled him as he watched her.

Here was a woman who had every right to walk away, to leave him and his family, and yet she'd stayed. She helped each of them with her quiet presence as the wait became more and more difficult.

He'd been so harsh with her earlier. He hadn't meant to be, he was so damn frustrated with the press and their constant digging into her life. But he hadn't been fair to her. Somehow he'd find a way to make it up to her.

Finally, at four a.m., Hassan walked in the door with another doctor.

His mother practically jumped off the cot, and Catherine was by her side in a second. Exhaustion lined her face. Malik and his brothers closed in around the women. If it was bad news, they needed to be there for their mother.

"He's out of danger," Hassan said.

A collective sigh of relief filled the room, and his mother sagged against him.

"He'll be okay?" Anna asked, her voice tired yet hopeful.

"Yes," the other doctor spoke up. "It was a warning sign. He needs to rest and follow my orders."

"What orders?" Malik asked, looking from the white-haired doctor to his brother.

The doctor shook his head. "I figured he hadn't mentioned anything to the family. The man is as stubborn as his father was."

"Like another man I know," Catherine whispered.

Malik fought against smiling at her words. This wasn't the time to be amused. "Tell us what we need to know."

"Well, it was a minor heart attack, nothing he can't recover from. He needs to take a backseat in running the country, to slow down, exercise, and eliminate some of the stress."

"I will see to it," Malik said.

The doctor nodded, then looked at Hassan. "I suggest all of you go home and get some rest. King Jamal won't be settled into a room for another few hours as we finish up the rest of our testing."

"Can I see him for a moment before I leave, please?" Anna asked.

Hassan nodded, took his mother's arm, and led her from the room, with the other doctor in the lead.

Malik paced the room until his mother returned. Her lips turned up, and she gave them all a little smile. "He's resting comfortably, and the doctor is right," Anna spoke up. "Let's go home and rest." Anna threaded her arm through Rafi's. Malik and Catherine and his remaining brothers followed them out of the waiting room, only to be met by his minister of information.

Omar began speaking rapidly in Arabic. Malik grimaced, and his brothers' and mother's expressions tightened.

"Go home. I'll take care of this. It's my job," Malik said, then turned to Samir and talked to him in a low tone before he waved Omar away.

"What is it?" Catherine asked.

"I'm sorry, Catherine, that was rude of us," Anna said.

Catherine waved a hand as if she hadn't been left out of the conversation. He needed to speak to Omar about using English until Catherine learned more of their language. Until that time, he would make sure someone translated for her.

Malik glanced at his mother. She was worn out, and Catherine? Catherine glanced from one person to the next, her hands clenched at her side, waiting for an answer.

"It's the paparazzi," Khalid said finally.

"They want to know what condition Father is in. Malik will address them," Rafi said.

"And we're to go home," Hassan finished.

"Don't you have a spokesperson to do this?"

Khalid shook his head. "This must come from a family member or the people won't believe Father will get better."

Catherine looked at Malik. "Yes," he said to her unspoken question. "It has to come from me."

"But you're as exhausted as the rest of us."

Malik shook his head, and Omar approached once again, this time with a frown marring his forehead.

"Malik." She placed a hand on his arm as she spoke. "I'm not going to allow you to kill yourself. You need to rest. The press can wait."

Their gazes met, and his dark eyes softened. "Catherine," he started.

"This is no place for you, I don't think—" started his minister.

"You're not thinking," she said before he could finish. "Everyone needs rest. We've been here all night, as I'm sure you're aware. In a few hours, Malik can make a statement about his father. The press will be satisfied with that."

"An announcement needs to be made now." The man puffed out his chest.

Catherine stared at him. Malik almost burst out laughing. She wasn't going to back down; he could see it in the way her chin jutted up and her eyes hardened.

"No, it doesn't," she countered. "Since you're the minister of information, isn't it your job to inform the press of certain events? You can tell the press that Malik will make a full statement this afternoon after he's had some rest. The king is resting comfortably. That's all that needs to be said. It's unfair to expect Malik to face the press now."

"You have no right here, woman."

His tone was dismissive, and the way he spit out the word *woman* raised the hair on Malik's neck. He was about to say something when Catherine let out a puff of breath. Her back stiffened and she glared at the minister.

"Since everyone believes I'm Malik's fiancée, I would say it gives me every right. No one in the family needs this crap right now, so back off."

Male laughter followed her statement. Damn, his woman could handle herself.

"I—" the minister sputtered.

"Enough," Malik spoke. He cupped Catherine's chin in his palm and tilted her face up. Never, outside of his family, had someone defended him or his family so passionately. His heart swelled. He'd picked well. "Catherine is my fiancée and will be given the respect she deserves. She's within her rights, and now is not the time for me or anyone in the family to address the press. Set up a press conference for this afternoon."

"But, Your Highness … "

"Don't contradict me, Omar. I'll meet you in my office at two to discuss the announcement." With that, Malik slipped an arm around Catherine's waist and led her away from Omar.

"You're stuck now," he whispered in her ear.

"Stuck?"

"Yes. You've just announced you're my intended to me, my minister, and my family." A grin overtook his lips. Maybe this wasn't the way he wanted to gain a fiancée, but he was happy it was Catherine.

16

Catherine couldn't settle down in her room once they'd arrived back at the palace. Malik's words vibrated in her mind. She didn't feel stuck in the situation, and it didn't bother her as she thought it would.

At the time, she'd wondered what she was doing confronting Malik's minister of information, and in an instant she knew. She was protecting Malik, a man she cared about. A man who had taken a piece of her heart and now held it. She was no longer frightened of her feelings for him. And she had more or less accepted being engaged to him for now.

Sooner or later, the press would ferret out more information about her parents and they would talk, then there was Jamie and … what? Really, those were the only two dark secrets in her life. Jamie actually wasn't a secret, she just hadn't told Malik about him. As for her parents … she let out a sigh. She'd walked away from them, their lavish lifestyle, and their need to keep feeding the paparazzi when she was eighteen. She'd severed all contact with them, and she wanted to keep it that way.

Pacing around her room, she decided nothing else mattered but Malik and his family. They needed her right now. When things calmed down, they could figure out how to extract her from the family, and all of them could go on with their lives.

She stopped her pacing in front of the balcony doors, then pushed them open and stepped out. Maybe some fresh air would clear her head and help her relax. The sun was just rising, the sky a beautiful combination of blue, pink, and yellow. Without thought, she turned and made her way to Malik's room. The lights were on.

He'd commented earlier there was a lot to do, but she'd insisted he rest. It wasn't fair to expect him to jump right into his father's role, even if his minister thought it would be best.

Did Malik's minister have the crown prince's best interests in mind? She'd never understood putting affairs of the state ahead of personal health. Just like she never understood why Jamie continued to perform when he should have been in the hospital. Or why her parents continued their lavish lifestyle without money.

Drawing level with Malik's room, she saw the balcony doors were open, so she leaned in. She didn't see him anywhere. "Malik," Catherine called softly as she stepped into the room. Silence greeted her.

Should she leave? She couldn't. She needed to make sure he was okay. He'd been tired and worn down after the events of the last twenty-four hours and the run-in with his minister of information and the other ministers when the family had returned to the palace.

Quietly, she padded across the room and peeked into his bedroom. The bed was empty and the bathroom door stood wide open. No water or noises. Where was he? Images of Jamal's heart attack flashed in her mind. She forced herself not to panic.

She turned, then took a step and froze. Malik was sprawled out on the sofa, sound asleep. Papers littered his chest and floor.

Her heart leaped as she gazed at him. His face showed lines of strain and a vulnerability she hadn't seen before. The events from the last day had caught up with him.

She bent down and gathered up the papers from the floor, putting them together in a neat stack before setting them on the table. Then she did the same with the ones on his chest.

Her fingers shook as she lifted each piece of paper. She didn't want to wake him. Out of all of them, he was probably the one who most needed sleep. Guilt crept into her bones. If she hadn't run away Saturday night, then would any of this have happened?

After adding the papers to the pile, she switched off the

overhead lights. No sense in leaving them on. If other people saw them, they might disturb him. She strode back into his bedroom to grab the colorful quilt off his bed and carried it back into the sitting room, careful not to trip over it.

Trying to be quiet, she arranged the quilt over him so he wouldn't get cold. She went still when he stirred, afraid she'd wake him if she moved. But he didn't wake, he only shifted his position.

She let out a sigh. Then jumped when someone knocked softly on the door. Her first instinct was to run so no one saw she was in his room. No. She glanced at Malik and his peaceful expression. It was the first time she'd seen him that relaxed. She could handle this without waking him. She was determined Malik not be disturbed.

The knock sounded again and Malik shifted, spurring her into action. She hurried to the door and opened it an inch. Catherine was relieved to see Hassan standing there and not the minister of information. She slipped out of the room.

"He's sleeping."

"Good. I was going to offer him a sleeping pill, even though I knew he probably wouldn't take it." He paused and gazed at her. "Do you need one?"

"No. I couldn't settle down until I was sure Malik was settled." She hadn't even realized how true the words were until she spoke them aloud. "Can you stop anyone from disturbing him for a few hours?"

"I'll take care of it." Hassan nodded.

"Especially the minister of information."

Hassan's lips twitched. "Yes, definitely."

"Thank you."

"I should be thanking you," Hassan said as he placed his hand on her arm.

"Why?" Lord, his family was so polite and kind. It wasn't what she was used to.

"Because you're good for him and for the family." He squeezed her arm and then walked away.

Catherine shook her head, and then slipped back into Malik's room. She should leave, but she couldn't. Her heart was screaming at her to stay and make sure Malik slept, while her brain, on the contrary, told her she should leave. Padding across the room, she stared at herself in the mirror.

"What the hell are you doing?" she whispered, but of course there was no answer. Her heart was winning the fight with her brain. She tiptoed back over to where Malik slept and quietly said, "Sleep well." Then she brushed a kiss over his forehead. This was madness, she reminded herself as she walked into his bedroom and climbed into his bed. Madness to remain in his room, crazy to climb into his bed, but she had to be close to him. Her heart demanded it.

Malik turned and stretched his cramped muscles. The last thing he remembered was reading the speech one of his ministers had given him. He opened his eyes and looked at his watch. It was almost eleven. He'd slept four hours. How had that happened?

He started to sit up, but the quilt covering him hampered his efforts. Someone had been in his room. Footsteps sounded from his bedroom, and hastily he lay back down and closed his eyes, curious to see who was in his room.

Catherine's scent of honey floated over to him, and in an instant he realized she was the one who had covered him. He waited to see what she would do. He barely breathed, afraid of giving himself away.

"Malik," she said, her voice quiet and tender.

He didn't move, curious to see if she'd wake him with a kiss.

"Darn it. I hate to wake you, but Hassan just texted me and your ministers are chomping at the bit." Her soft fingers curled around his shoulder and shook him. "Malik, you need to wake up." Her voice was louder this time.

Malik opened his eyes and smiled at her. "You're a nice sight to wake up to."

A blush rose to her cheeks, and unable to help himself, he cupped the back of her neck and brought her down for a kiss. Her lips were as soft as he remembered and just as sweet. He deepened the kiss, their tongues doing an intricate mating dance, until a knock sounded at his door and broke the mood. Catherine pulled away from him, breathing heavily.

"I need to go."

"Stay." He captured her hand.

"I shouldn't be here," she said, her eyes wide, her lips swollen from his kiss.

"This is where you belong. In my arms, in my bed, in my home. Don't let anyone tell you otherwise." His erection pressed against his pants. If they had more time, he'd take her to bed and show her his dominant ways. A knock sounded again. With swift movements, he rose to his feet and wrapped the quilt around her before moving to the door. This way she didn't have to object.

A few hours later, Malik paced the room, his traditional robe of white, gold, and red slapping around his feet. He was nervous. It wasn't like he hadn't addressed his people before, but today was different. He would update them on his father's condition, which was stable, thank God. Today, his people would look for him to lead. Today, he would take a major step toward becoming the next king.

Did he really want this? The question shocked him. He'd been raised to do this; he'd always known he was destined to be king. Some day. He'd figured it was further in the future, but his father's heart attack changed everything.

Movement caught his attention, yanking him out of his thoughts. He glanced up to see Catherine, and his world brightened. If one good thing had come out of his father's illness, it was that Catherine had agreed to stay.

It amazed him how important to him she'd become in such a short time. He continued to pace, watching her out of the corner of his eyes, while he went through the speech he was about to make, over and over again.

"You'll be fine." Catherine's soft voice soothed him and stopped his restless movement. She wore a simple white dress with short sleeves, and the fabric fell around her ankles. What caught his attention was the sash of the royal colors. His mother must have given it to her and convinced her to wear it without her knowing what it meant.

"Yes, I will." But would he? So much was changing, and fast.

"Malik." She laid a hand on his arm. Her warmth surrounded him. "Breathe and relax. Your father is recovering."

He nodded. Yes, his father was recovering, quite rapidly. He was already asking to leave the hospital and giving Malik advice on how to handle the ministers. Malik had convinced his dad to stay for another twenty-four hours and let the doctors make sure there was no major damage to his heart.

"Your people love you," she continued. "The speech itself is a formality to let everyone know Jamal is fine. Plus, you're more than capable of stepping into his shoes."

He drew her into his arms. "They're very big shoes to fill," he whispered. How was it he could express his misgivings to Catherine, but not to his family? What was it about her?

"Agreed, but if anyone can do it, you can."

Her confidence in him made his ego swell. "You really believe that, don't you?" He knew his family supported him, but to have Catherine believe in him so unconditionally was a new experience. Most women he'd dated before never seemed to support him like she did or even to think much about what his position entailed.

"I do." She brushed her fingers over his cheek. "There is no one I believe in more at this moment than you. You are the crown prince of Bashir. You're stepping up to do what you need to do, for your people, your country, your family, and your father. You may not feel ready, but you are."

He grimaced. She saw so much. Did others see what she did? He hated to think his ministers were reading him as well as she was. He couldn't be weak in front of his ministers, as they only respected strength. "Is it that obvious?"

"No." Her lips tilted up. "I'm good at reading people. It's the artist in me."

"Be with me on the balcony as I make the speech." He'd tried to convince her earlier to be with him, but she'd refused. But he wanted her there. She helped keep his nerves at bay, and he wanted to show his people the woman he wanted to become the next queen.

"It's not my place." She ducked her head but didn't try to escape his embrace. That was progress.

"I can't think of a better place for you to be than at my

side. You are to be my crown princess." And she was quickly becoming very important to him.

"Malik," she started, lifting her chin.

He slid his hands to her hips and turned her so his back faced the room and she was shielded from prying eyes.

"What are you doing?" Her hands fluttered to his shoulders.

"This." He lowered his head and captured her lips. She tasted of sweetness and light, pure Catherine—his strength, his courage, his woman. Wanting to keep the kiss light, he lifted his head.

Her eyes flared with desire, and he wanted to kiss her again, the way a lover kissed another. Slow, long, and hot. He wanted her more and more with each passing minute.

"Did that help?" she asked, as she traced his jaw with her fingers, her touch making his skin tingle with pleasure.

"Yes." And it had. There was something freeing about having his woman in his arms. "Later, I'm going to explore every part of your body while I have you tied to my bed." A shiver shook her body as her eyes widened and desire blazed in them.

"It's almost time," his minister of information interrupted.

Malik inclined his head and waited until the man retreated. Ever since Omar had insulted Catherine earlier that morning, Malik had watched his minister with new eyes. What else was the man doing that he didn't know about? "You'll be with my family?" His mother and brothers would be in the adjoining room, within sight of the people.

"Yes."

"Good." He brushed his lips over her cheek, breathing in her scent, then he took a step back and released her from his embrace.

"You'll knock them dead," she said, before stepping around him and joining his family.

17

Catherine gnawed on her lower lip as she watched Malik from her vantage point. He looked so handsome in the traditional robe and so right addressing his people. She was proud of him.

She listened to his words and scanned the crowds below. It was obvious the people thought the world of the royal family and the crown prince. They cheered when Malik told them his father's heart attack was minor and he was recovering quickly. Then they cheered again when he said he would be taking a more active role in running the country during this crisis. A big cheer went up when he made the announcement that he'd found his future crown princess.

Her breath caught in her throat when Malik turned. He'd tried earlier to convince her to join him, but she didn't want to be in the spotlight. She sighed; there was no way to keep their engagement in the dark, especially since it was already in all the papers.

Khalid nudged her in the back, and in a trance she moved to Malik's side, taking his outstretched hand. She was setting herself up for heartbreak, but she couldn't avoid it. She was falling for this man. He had facets that she itched to explore. Maybe she could overcome her past with him by her side.

When he tugged her to his side, he dropped a light kiss against her lips. The applause and cheering became deafening. Then, still holding her hand, Malik finished his speech. "Wave," he whispered when he'd finished.

Together, they waved to the crowd, who continued to cheer, even as she and Malik disappeared from sight.

His family was waiting for them, and Anna smiled at Catherine. "That was a lovely thing to do."

"What?" she asked.

"To go to Malik's side, to acknowledge you will be our crown princess, and waving to the people. You've made their day." There was approval and acceptance in Anna's voice.

Catherine's cheeks grew hot. Malik had told her to wave, and she had. It was just a friendly gesture, wasn't it? Then she thought about the kiss. "Did I make some sort of mistake in waving or the kiss?"

"Not at all," said Hassan.

"Nope," added Rafi.

"In fact," Khalid said, taking her hand in his, "by joining Malik, the kiss, and the wave, you've publicly acknowledged the engagement. The press will be frantic now." He hesitated, and then added, "In a good way."

Catherine closed her eyes when her stomach dropped to her feet at Khalid's words. Life would be perfect without the press. Well, she'd stepped into the fire all by herself this time. Maybe the fake engagement would take some of the pressure off Malik.

Later that evening, Catherine stood outside her room on the balcony. She loved this time of night. Not too hot and not too cold.

"Are you okay?" Malik's voice drifted over to her. She turned her head to see him lounging against the railing, watching her.

"Yes." She let out a sigh. "You could have told me what was going to happen today before I stepped to your side."

"I didn't want you bolting." He sauntered over to her and lifted his hand, and his fingers caressed her cheek before slipping behind her neck.

"You think you know me so well." The gesture calmed her nerves.

"I do." His lips found hers.

Catherine sank into his kiss, her lips parting to allow his tongue to thrust into her waiting mouth.

Hot tendrils of desire wove their way through her body and around her until her skin felt as if it would burst from need. She broke the kiss and gazed up at Malik. "I want you."

His eyes darkened. And the next thing she knew she was

in his arms, and he was striding into her room. The balcony doors slammed shut as he kicked them before he made his way into her bedroom.

She was crazy, that's all there was to it. She was getting in deeper rather than pushing Malik away, but she didn't want to push him away. Catherine wanted to feel his lips on hers, his body against hers, his passion igniting hers.

He lowered her to her feet, his fingers at the tie of her robe. He loosened it, and he sucked in a breath. She grinned.

"You are exquisite," he whispered, pushing the fabric from her shoulders. She hadn't bothered to dress after her shower. Her body was completely exposed to him. "Tonight, you are mine."

He lifted her onto the mattress, positioning her in the middle of the bed before he removed his own robe.

Her breath caught in her throat. Lord, he was magnificent. His body was fit and toned. Dark hair trailed down his chest to where it disappeared beneath the white briefs he wore. His penis pushed against the fabric.

"Ummm." She didn't know what to say. She wanted him, but was suddenly shy.

"Shhh." He leaned over and kissed her gently on the mouth. "Let me take care of you."

She tilted her head, puzzled, until he grinned and began kissing and licking her neck. Her head arched back, giving him more access. His lips were so soft, and his tongue tickled as he nibbled his way down to her throat.

Catherine's nerves danced to life under Malik's talented mouth. His lips caressed the base of her throat, sliding lower, he lapped at her left nipple. Her mouth fell open with the sensation of his tongue against her breast, as he moved to the right. Shivers of pleasure flowed through her nipples straight to her center.

Without thought, she tangled her hands in his hair, holding him to her. His head rose, and he stared down at her. "No touching."

"What?" He couldn't be serious.

Malik rolled off the mattress, and before she could form a question, he was back, pulling her arms over her head. Soft fabric looped around her wrists. Catherine tilted her head up. He'd taken the belt off his robe and was tying her up.

Her breath caught in her throat. Malik gazed into her eyes. Desire, want, and need flared in his dark depths. The tiny flickers of gold in his eyes sparked with fire and heat.

"Now you are at my mercy." His voice was low and husky.

She tugged at her bonds. They were firm, but not painful. Anticipation licked through her veins, but she wasn't stupid. "Do I need a safeword?"

His eyes darkened further. "Princess," he murmured.

"What?" Did he say what she thought he had?

"Princess is your safeword." He grinned. "But you won't need it."

Malik moved down her body until his lips caressed her

stomach, and then he moved lower. His palms were warm against her inner thighs as he pushed her legs apart and continued his journey.

Her skin danced as he nipped and licked his way between her thighs. Then he swiped his tongue over her outer lips.

"Malik," she cried his name, her hips rising from the mattress.

"Sweet," he whispered. His fingers worked their way over the top of her slit, and maneuvered over her skin until he was able to part her outer lips, exposing her to him.

When he licked her this time, Catherine closed her eyes on a moan at the sensations coursing their way through her body. Oh, dear Lord. Then he closed his mouth over her clit and sucked.

She thrashed against the mattress, her muscles tightening. It was overwhelming, the feeling of his mouth on her, his tongue playing with that little bundle of nerves. Her senses were on overload.

Malik held Catherine's thrashing body easily. She tasted so good. Like honey and spice rolled into one sweet treat. He kept an eye on her as he licked, sucked, and nipped at her slit.

Her body was flushed; she'd closed her eyes and panted. Good, aroused and on edge. That's how he wanted her. He kept tormenting her as he slid his right hand over her inner thigh.

More honey flowed from her, she was so wet and so

ready. His dick swelled. No, this was for her. He'd promised her he'd kiss her all over, and he was going to fulfill that promise, but first … He slid two fingers into her core.

Her hips bucked as her feet tried to find purchase on the mattress. Wasn't going to happen, not with him between her legs, keeping her open to him. He lifted his head.

"You are so wet and tasty."

"Too much," she whispered, her fingers curled into her palms.

"Not enough." He blew against her mound and she let out a moan. "Let go, my princess. Let me give you the pleasure you deserve."

He lowered his head. Her hips jerked as he moved his fingers within her core, while he continued to use his tongue against the sensitive bundle of nerves. She was so sweet, so sexy, so … his. Her muscles tightened around his fingers.

Oh, yes, she was close. He doubled his efforts, his fingers finding that special spot inside her. The second he pressed his fingers against her G-spot, she cried out and her body shuddered as she climaxed.

He grinned against her skin, his tongue now smoothing over her hot button rather than arousing it. Malik lifted his head, watching her body float down from her orgasm. She was so damn beautiful. Her muscles still clenched his fingers deep within her.

She opened her eyes and their gazes clashed. Her blue eyes were languid with satisfaction. But he wanted more. Carefully, he slipped his fingers from her pussy.

"So beautiful," he whispered, and he kissed his way down her left leg, and then up her right leg. His cock strained with need, but he ignored it. This was for her. This was her night. He would get his later.

When he kissed his way back up her body, his lips captured hers. Her body bucked against his, but she didn't try to pull away; instead, she kissed him back.

He trailed his fingers back to her slit as they kissed. She was still wet. He slid his digits into her again. Her body bucked harder as muscles tightened around his fingers.

Malik raised his head and stared into her eyes. "Again," he whispered.

18

Catherine woke to someone knocking on her door. Malik? She turned her head, but she was alone in bed. Malik? Her heart raced. No, he would use the balcony doors, as he had last night when he'd swept into her room and carried her to bed.

Her core tightened with the memory of all the wicked things he'd done with his mouth last night. She vaguely remembered his kissing her early this morning, telling her he was going back to his room and for her to get some sleep.

Looking at the clock, she let out a groan. It was seven. She hadn't fallen asleep until five. She found her robe on the chair and slipped it on. Her face warmed, remembering the way Malik had tied her wrists. Shaking her head, she walked to the outer room and opened the door. A woman swept through the doorway, almost knocking Catherine down.

"Miss Taylor, you should be dressed. Where is your maid? We have so much to do today. Fittings, etiquette, history lessons, protocol lessons. We'll never fit it all in."

Catherine rubbed her eyes as her brain tried to make sense of what the woman was saying. "Who are you?"

"I'm your liaison." She looked at the door Catherine still held open. "Oh, good, the dressmakers are here. Let's get started."

Three hours later, Catherine escaped from the sitting room into her bedroom, slamming the door between herself and that woman. Enough was enough. She'd been poked and prodded for hours by Lillianna, as she said her name was. She had been sent by the minister of information to help Catherine transition into the royal family, and they had a lot of work to do.

This whole thing was an unnecessary exercise. It was a fake engagement. A tiny part of her whispered it could be real if she said the right words to Malik, but she shushed the voice. She'd play her part until the mural was done, and that was it. But her heart pounded at the thought of breaking her rules and just going for it with Malik.

Catherine sighed as she pulled on a pair of her favorite jeans and a blouse. While it might not be dignified, she was going to sneak out, again. Another minute with Lillianna and she was going to strangle her. Catherine could give the woman lessons in protocol, how to dress, and beyond. All things she'd learned as a child from her parents. Things she'd rather not go over again.

Slipping out the balcony doors, she jogged down the back staircase and through a door into the lower level. She asked one of the staff to have Samir bring a car around. Catherine cautiously made her way to the breakfast room and peeked around the door.

Oh, good, no one was there. She slipped into the room and found her travel mug on the counter—where it sat waiting for her every morning. Filled it from the hot pot sitting on the counter, then hightailed it out of there. Samir pulled up as she came out the front door. Within a minute, she was inside the car, and they were on the way to the hospital. Just because she was Malik's fiancée didn't mean she was going to give up her independence, style, and who she was.

"One more, please," the children cried as they clamored for another story.

Catherine smiled. Upon arriving at the hospital, she realized all her supplies were still at the palace. Instead of going back or sending Samir after them, she decided to read stories to the kids. That was where Hassan had found her a few minutes ago. "Sorry, kids." Hassan had informed her she needed to get back to the palace before all hell broke loose. "I promised Dr. Hassan I'd stop after this last story." She glanced at the clock on the wall. It was after three, and she'd been with the kids since eleven that morning.

The kids let out a groan, but they didn't argue. Instead,

they all moved back to their beds, and Catherine made sure to visit each child before she left.

Hassan stood waiting just outside the door. "How much trouble am I in?" she asked.

He laughed. "Your barracuda liaison is threatening to tear you apart, the minister of information is having fits, Malik—who is not upset at all—is trying to deal with them both, and my sainted mother, who I sent home an hour ago, laughs even harder each time I've spoken with her."

Catherine had stopped by Jamal's room when she first came in, but Anna had been there, holding hands with her husband and talking. She hadn't wanted to disturb them. "At least I have one person on my side." She could see Anna laughing at the situation, and it warmed her heart.

"More than one." Hassan touched her shoulder. "Don't let them get you down, Catherine. Keep doing what you're doing now. They'll learn."

"Thanks, Hassan." They stopped in the reception area. She didn't see Samir anywhere. Then Hassan's pager went off.

"Go," she said.

"But Samir isn't here."

"He'll be here in a minute. Your patients need you. Now, shoo."

Hassan smiled before walking away.

Catherine paced the area waiting for Samir, all the while trying to formulate a plan for dealing with Lillianna and the minister of information. A car pulled up, and Catherine stepped outside. Warning bells went off in her head. That wasn't Samir. Before she could turn, someone grabbed her from behind.

19

Malik listened to Omar drone on about how Catherine wasn't committed to being his consort and how she needed to be at the palace, not at the hospital.

"Catherine is very committed to her work and the children. I will not stand in her way. She'll be fine." Deep in his gut, he was aware of Catherine's hidden depths. He wasn't worried about her knowing which knife to use at a state dinner. None of that was important.

He glanced up as the door to his office opened. His mother's pale face brought him to his feet and across the room.

"Father?" he asked, his heart constricting.

"He's fine. It's Catherine."

Malik's heart stopped. He didn't question his mother, his only thought was to get to Catherine. He swept by her and down the hallway, ignoring his minister of information. He rushed out of the house and jumped into the waiting car. Within seconds of the car pulling away, his cell phone rang. He pulled it out to see his mother's number.

"Sorry, Mother. I need—"

"Quiet, son. Catherine is okay, I'll let Hassan fill you in, but I didn't want you running into a situation unknown."

"What happened?" His heart still pounded in his chest, but his mother's words helped him calm down a little.

"I'm not sure. One of the nurses called because Catherine was injured, not badly. I could hear Catherine saying it wasn't necessary, but Hassan wanted you there."

He blew out a breath. If Hassan hadn't called, it couldn't be too bad. "Thank you, Mother. I'll call as soon as I find out what is going on." Malik hung up as the car pulled up to the hospital entrance. Ignoring the police, press, and his bodyguards, he strode into the hospital.

Samir waited inside the doors. "She's this way." Samir gestured to the emergency room, and Malik nodded and followed him. "You should be aware she was attacked, Your Highness."

"What?" Malik's heart stopped beating as he swept into the room, his dark gaze focused in on her as she argued with his brother. His heart started beating again, and he fought against pulling her into his arms.

"I'm all right, Hassan," Catherine said, trying to sit up.

"I'll be the judge of that. Does your head hurt?"

"Of course it does." She rolled her eyes. "I head-butted the guy."

"Did you black out?"

"No, just stunned myself."

Hassan flashed a light into one of her eyes, then the other. "I'm worried about your head. I'd like to do a CAT scan."

"I don't think it's necessary," she protested.

"You'll do as my brother says," Malik said, using his best Dom voice and crossing his arms over his chest.

"Great, just what I need, two of them," Catherine said.

The nurse in the room let out a laugh, then stifled it as Malik turned and looked at her. "Excuse me," she said, and fled.

"You've frightened my only ally out of the room." Catherine glared at him.

Malik turned to her. His gaze took in the small bump on her forehead, scratches on her arms, and the mutinous expression on her face.

"It's a precaution, Catherine," Hassan intervened.

"An unnecessary test."

"You've been attacked and injured." Malik looked at his brother. "Was the person caught?"

"No. He jumped into the car after Catherine head-butted him."

"I see. I will go have a talk with Samir about his duty."

"You will not." Catherine sat up and swung her legs over the side of the bed.

"Lie back down," Malik ordered.

"No." Catherine lifted her chin and looked him in the eye. "Samir is not at fault. He went to get the car as usual. I wasn't paying attention, and when a similar vehicle pulled up, I just assumed it was the right one. Blame me." Then she turned to his brother. "I'm fine. I don't need a CAT scan. You have other patients who need you. Go attend them." She stood and faced Malik. "I'm going back to the palace now." She marched past them and out of the room.

"Stubborn woman," Malik said, staring after Catherine. His heart was finally calming down.

"Yes," his brother agreed.

"How hurt is she?" He'd go after her in a minute. Besides, Samir was right outside the door, and he wouldn't let her get very far or leave the hospital without him.

"Maybe a mild concussion but no loss of consciousness. I'd wake her every few hours tonight to be on the safe side. She'll probably be a little sore tomorrow and bruised where the guy grabbed her. From what I was told, she fought the guy when she realized what was happening."

Malik swore. "You didn't witness it?"

"No. A couple of other employees on break saw the altercation and went to aid her."

"She's supposed to be looked after and not left alone. Why didn't you stay with her?" Anger filled him—at his brother, the staff, Samir, himself. This was his fault. He should have come after her this morning instead of letting her spend the day with the children.

Hassan held up his hands. "First off, I was paged, and second, I left her in the reception area to wait for Samir. I didn't realize she'd go outside alone."

"Sorry." Malik tried to rein in his temper. "Not your fault. There should have been another guard with her. Where was he?"

Hassan shrugged. "Don't know. I escorted her from the children's ward to reception." He glanced at the empty doorway. "If I were you, I'd go find Catherine before she leaves the hospital on her own."

"She won't. Samir is watching her."

"Are you sure?"

Malik swore and took off after Catherine. The woman was apt at losing her security detail. Where had she learned to do that?

Catherine sank down onto the overstuffed sofa in an empty waiting room, forcing her body to relax. Her anger with Hassan and Malik had lasted all of two minutes after she had stormed out of the room. Being angry made her head hurt, and it hurt enough already. Leaning her head back, she closed her eyes. In a few minutes she'd ask Samir to take her to the palace, but for the moment she wanted some peace and quiet.

Soft footsteps paused outside the door, and she kept her eyes closed. "Go away," she said. The unique smell of sandalwood tickled her nose as Malik walked into the room. She had to fight against throwing herself into his arms. She wasn't a damsel in distress. She'd fought off her attacker, and from the whispers of the nurses, the man had been bleeding pretty badly. One day as the future crown princess and already someone had tried to kidnap her.

"Maybe you should listen to my brother and spend the night here."

"It's just a headache." With another six-foot pain in the butt standing too close. "Give me two aspirin, and let me get some sleep. I'll be fine."

"So fine you're sitting here with your eyes closed."

A sigh slipped from her lips. She didn't want to fight with him, but she wasn't going to stay in the hospital. Too many memories. A shiver crept up her spine. While she was working or spending time with the kids it didn't bother her, but she was not going to spend the night.

"Malik, I don't want to argue with you. I just want to go back to the palace and fall into my bed." Silence followed her words. "Please," she added.

The air stirred around her, then she was lifted into his arms. "Malik?" She pried her eyes open and entwined her arms around his neck.

"Shh, lay your head on my shoulder and be quiet, before I decide having you admitted to the hospital is better than this lunacy." His voice was soft and tender.

Catherine kept her mouth shut and relaxed into his hold. Her head rested against his shoulder as he carried her out of the hospital to the waiting car. She didn't want to think of how they looked or what other people saw, especially any press hanging around. Instead, she concentrated on the complex man holding her.

His scent, sandalwood and pure masculinity, teased her senses. His arms were strong and sure, and he made her feel safe. Safer than she'd felt in a long time. Not since she was a small child had she had this contented, secure feeling. His deep voice was subdued when he spoke to Samir, but she didn't open her eyes.

She waited for Malik to lower her to her feet, but he didn't. He somehow managed to get them both settled into the car, with her on his lap. Catherine let out another sigh, one of satisfaction, and she snuggled into his embrace.

This is nice, she thought. Then she drifted off.

❧ 20 ❧

Malik took a deep breath as Catherine relaxed against him and her breathing became even and regular. She was asleep. He glanced at his watch, noting the time when he'd have to wake her.

He was torn between reading her the riot act, taking her to his bed and never letting her out, or spanking her butt until it was bright red. Who was he kidding? This woman stripped all his defenses, and he couldn't even stay angry with her. Concerned, but not angry.

Glancing down, he noted how pale her face was. Who in the world would want to hurt her? To kidnap her? He'd only made the official announcement of their engagement yesterday. Was this a crime of opportunity? It seemed like it. There was no way it could have been planned. Or could it? Catherine was always at the hospital working on the mural, or with the kids, and she usually left at the same time each day.

He'd make sure his private security officers got to the bottom of this. Samir was already on the phone to Khalid; as head of security, he'd find out what was going on. Malik tightened his arms around Catherine. "I won't let anyone hurt you," he whispered, pressing a kiss to the top of her head.

His mother was waiting when they pulled up to the palace. She frowned when Malik emerged from the car, carrying a sleeping Catherine. "Shouldn't she be in the hospital?" she asked in hushed tones.

"Yes, but she refused to stay." He swept into the palace, up the stairs, and into his bedroom.

"Is this wise?" his mother asked as she followed him.

"I'm not letting her out of my sight." He lay Catherine gently on the bed before facing his mother. "According to Hassan, she might have a mild concussion and some bruises."

"I'll send a maid to undress her." His mother touched his arm. "Your father is doing much better. I'll go back and visit him later tonight."

"Good." One less family member to worry about.

"It's very good." His mother smiled.

When his mother left the room, he turned to Catherine. She looked good in his bed. All he needed to do now was convince her to stay there.

Malik undressed and put on a robe. He maneuvered one

of the overstuffed chairs closer to the bed, grabbed the reports he needed to read, and sat down. Instead of reading, he stared at Catherine.

He'd almost lost her today. A tremor shook his body. Tossing the report in his hand aside, he leaned forward, elbows on knees. They hadn't known each other long, but he couldn't see a life without her in it. Her past didn't matter; he'd read the dossier Khalid had provided on her. While it had the highlights, it hadn't gone into a lot of detail, and Malik didn't care. His Catherine was sweet, caring, and his.

He smiled. She had fought her attacker, and he'd have to ask her about that. He admitted he didn't think she could hurt a fly, yet she'd protected herself. All this coming on the heels of his father's heart attack had Malik wondering if a political coup was in the making.

Were the tribal leaders working to gain ground? He didn't think so, but he'd have to make it a point to meet with them. To calm their fears. Catherine shifted, shaking Malik out of his thoughts. He'd promised to protect her, yet today she'd been hurt. He had already talked with Samir. There had been nothing out of the ordinary today. Hassan had been with Catherine, and Samir had gone to get the car.

Who was watching them? He ran his hand over his face, trying to erase the exhaustion. He was doubling her guards. She wasn't going to like it, but he would make sure she was safe.

Malik glanced at the clock. In another hour he'd wake her up to check on her, but in the meantime he could get some work done. But after twenty minutes of reading the same four lines, he shook his head.

He set the report aside again, removed his robe, and slipped into bed beside Catherine. Malik turned on his side and slipped his arm over her waist. Catherine wiggled and then snuggled closer to him.

Malik closed his eyes. This is where he wanted to be.

Catherine woke slowly, squinting at the light streaming into her room. She'd overslept. Without thinking, she started to stretch. "Ouch," she said out loud as muscles protested.

"What is it?"

Her eyes widened at Malik's voice. He was on his elbow, gazing down at her. His eyes were filled with concern and worry, making his forehead wrinkle.

"Sore muscles, that's all. What are you doing in my room?"

"It's my room. Let me help you." He slipped his hand behind her back as she tried to sit up. Then he piled pillows behind her.

"Your room?" Lord, she was sore. Maybe it was time to exercise a bit more if the small exertion she'd had yesterday had caused this. The events of the previous afternoon came flooding back, including Malik waking her several times during the night, and she let out a groan.

"You're in pain. Coming home was a bad idea. You should have stayed in the hospital." Worry tinged his voice.

"Malik." She cupped his cheek. Stubble teased her skin before she let her arm fall back to her side. "I'll be fine. A little sore from the tussle with my attacker, but otherwise, I'm just peachy. Why am I in your room and your bed?"

"Because this is where you belong." The words were said with a quiet forcefulness.

Catherine thought she'd imagined it, but one look at the fierce protectiveness in Malik's eyes told her she hadn't. Her heart began to pound. Her proud warrior was upset he hadn't been there to protect her. Now he was going all dominant on her, in more ways than one.

"But," she started, only to be interrupted by a knock on his bedroom door.

"Enter," Malik said.

Hassan strode into the room. "Good, you're awake. How's the head?"

It was then Catherine realized she no longer had a headache. "Fine, no pain at all."

"Good. What about pain elsewhere?"

"She said her muscles hurt," Malik said.

"I can speak for myself." She glared at Malik, who just grinned at her. "Muscles that haven't been used in a while are a little sore. Nothing that getting up and moving won't cure."

"Absolutely not," Malik said.

"I'm not an invalid." His stern tone and look should upset her, but instead it caused her blood to heat.

"You will stay in bed."

"Is that a royal decree?" Damn, his dominant side was making her insides melt.

"I'll make it one."

"Excuse me," Hassan said, trying to smother his laughter. "As her doctor, I'd say that it's a good idea if she does get up and move around."

"See, the doctor agrees with me." Catherine folded her arms over her chest.

"Very well." Malik nodded in a very regal way, like it was his idea all along. "I'll get you a robe and call a maid to help you dress."

"I can dress myself."

"A maid or me. Your choice."

"Darn, overprotective male," Catherine muttered, and Hassan burst out laughing.

"I'll leave you two to work this out." He quickly left the room.

"So, what is your choice?" He stared at her, his arms over his chest, looking like he was sitting on a throne rather than on a bed.

Catherine let out a sigh. "Fine, summon a maid." Part of her enjoyed his protectiveness, but another reminded her she was an independent woman. She was used to taking care of herself.

"Thank you." Malik brushed a kiss over her cheek before he climbed out of bed.

Her mouth watered. He was only wearing a pair of white briefs, and they clung to his magnificent ass. Muscles played over his back as he picked up the robe sitting on the chair. He strode around the bed and held it up for her to slip into.

She slid out of bed, stood, and placed her arms into the robe. Malik's hands descended on her shoulders. "Don't ever scare me like that again." His warm breath teased her cheek.

"I didn't mean to." She belted the robe before turning in his hold. "I just reacted to the situation."

Malik lowered his forehead to rest on hers. "Something we need to discuss as well." He pulled her into his embrace.

His heart beat strong and sure under her ear. She relaxed into his embrace and allowed his warmth to soak into her skin.

"And later we'll discuss your punishment."

"What does that mean?" Catherine pulled back, her jaw dropping open. But Malik tapped her on the nose and stepped away before sauntering into the bathroom.

❦ 21 ❦

An hour later, Catherine made her way into the family breakfast room. She hadn't realized the time it was until she asked the maid. It was after nine in the morning. She'd slept close to fourteen hours, not surprising with all she'd been through in the last few days.

Glancing around the room, she was surprised to see Malik and his brothers around the table. She'd hoped Malik would be in his office, as she was still digesting his last comment about her punishment, but he wasn't. "Good morning."

Malik rose to his feet with another frown on his face. "Where is—"

"I dismissed the maid outside the door, so don't get all huffy on me." She took her seat next to him and poured herself some tea.

"How are you feeling?" Rafi asked.

"I'm fine." She smiled at him.

"He gets a polite, 'I'm fine,' but when I ask you yell at me," Malik said, taking her hand in his.

"Yes." She wasn't going to lie to him. Malik's concern warmed her heart, but when he started getting dominant toward her outside the bedroom, it made her hackles rise. "So, what is on the agenda for today?"

"We've been discussing that," Khalid said.

"And I've said no," Malik said.

"You're being stubborn," Rafi commented.

Catherine looked at Hassan, who shrugged his shoulders. "Malik is concerned what Khalid has suggested would be too much for you."

"What is with you three spilling information so easily?"

She turned to Malik. "And what has been suggested?"

"No. I'm not discussing it." Malik frowned at her. "You are not well enough."

"Stubborn male," she muttered, then turned her attention to Khalid. "Tell me."

"Sorry, brother," Khalid said with a laugh. "Some of the tribal leaders have come forward and want a meeting with Malik."

"But that's wonderful." She knew Malik had been worried about how the tribal leaders took the news of their fake engagement.

"It is," Rafi said. "But Malik won't meet with them."

"Why ever not?" She turned in her chair toward Malik.

"You must meet with them. This will give them a chance to talk with you."

"I will not risk your well-being," Malik said, his jaw tight.

Catherine waited, but Malik said no more, so she turned her attention to Rafi. "What is he talking about?"

"The tribal leaders have asked Malik to bring you to the meeting," Rafi said.

"So?" What was she missing? There had to be something. Warm fingers cupped her chin. Malik's dark eyes were filled with concern.

"The tribal leaders want the meeting in the desert. It would mean spending a night out there," Malik said.

Catherine inhaled. "A night in the desert?"

"Yes, you're getting over a concussion. I won't risk your health," Malik said, as his fingers caressed her cheek.

"I'm fine." She raised her free hand to his cheek. "Really, I am. A bit sore. Malik, you need to do this. If they want me with you, then I'll go willingly."

"I knew you were a woman of worth," Khalid said. "I'll start the process." He stood.

"I haven't said yes," Malik said, but his gaze never left her face.

"Formality," Rafi said.

Chairs scraped back and Catherine vaguely heard footsteps retreating.

"Are you sure?" Malik asked.

She nodded. "I want to see the desert. With everything

going on, it might just be the thing to tip the odds in your favor."

"Can you ride a horse?"

She grinned. "Yes, I can." She didn't tell him it had been a while.

"And you'll accept all security measures Khalid sees fit to implement and whomever he decides to send with us?"

She nodded.

"All right." He lowered his head until his forehead rested on hers.

Four hours later, Malik led the group on his black Arabian into the encampment the trial leaders had set up. It had taken them a little longer than normal because he'd insisted on stopping and resting.

Malik wasn't sure bringing Catherine out in the desert after her recent scare was such a good idea, but Khalid had assured him it was probably the safest place for her. Khalid had assigned a special security force, handpicked, including himself, plus he'd sent out a group ahead to set up their own tents and make sure everything was secure.

Malik stopped his horse, dismounted, and went to Catherine's horse. Without a word he helped her dismount. "How are you doing?" he asked.

"Good," she said. "I'm sure there will be a few muscles that will protest tomorrow when we ride back, but nothing major. Please relax." He reached up and unwound her headscarf. She glanced over his shoulder and her eyes widened.

Malik turned to see three of the tribal leaders with their wives standing there. Malik undid the fabric covering his face.

"Prince Malik," Faruq, one of the tribal leaders, said. "We are pleased you are here." All of them bowed.

"Faruq, Bassam, and Anwar, thank you for the invitation to meet with you." Malik slid his arm around Catherine's waist and pulled her to his side. "This is Catherine, my wife-to-be."

"Hello." Her voice was soft.

"We welcome you as well," Faruq said with a smile. "Come refresh yourselves." He gestured them toward the large fire pit with pillows scattered around.

"Thank you for your kindness and generosity." Malik guided Catherine over to the area and helped her sit on a pillow.

The wives scuttled off and returned with food and drinks as the men settled themselves. Catherine looked at Malik as the men were served.

"It's an old tradition," he whispered. "Men are served first."

She nodded. Anwar's wife knelt down next to Catherine, holding out a cup. "Thank you," Catherine said as she took the cup.

Malik lifted his cup and took a sip, then nodded at

Catherine, who did the same. He had explained a bit on the way out, but had forgotten about how old-fashioned the tribal leaders were. She'd picked up on it right away.

"As soon as you finish your refreshment, our wives will take your bride-to-be to your tent and we can talk," Bassam said.

Catherine stiffened beside him. Malik wished he could pull her into his arms, but the tribal leaders frowned upon public displays of affection. "I mean no disrespect, Bassam, but I prefer to keep Catherine with me as we talk."

Bassam shook his head.

"Prince Malik," Anwar started.

Malik held his hand up. "Please hear me out. I respect the old ways, I always have. But some recent events are why I want Catherine at my side." He outlined what had happened.

"And you believe we are responsible?" Bassam threw out his chest.

"Quiet, Bassam," Faruq said. "Prince Malik is within his rights to keep his woman near him for her protection."

"My protection," Catherine whispered.

Malik inclined his head.

"I do not like it," Bassam said. "Anwar?"

Anwar stared at Catherine. Malik wanted to tell her to lower her gaze, but this had to play out the way it did. Catherine wasn't a meek woman.

Anwar rubbed his chin. "Strong, and a brave woman. She stays."

Malik hadn't realized how tense he was until Anwar spoke. "Thank you. Now shall we discuss the matters at hand?"

Catherine stirred as male arms lifted her. She forced her eyes open. The men had talked all afternoon and into the evening. A fire had been lit in the pit and meat roasted over it. The food had been flavorful, and the conversation interesting.

The tribal leaders laid out their issues and Malik listened. He never dismissed anything they said, and those items he didn't have answers to he promised to look into. Somewhere along the line she'd fallen asleep.

"Malik?"

"Hello, my sleepy one." He grinned at her as he carried her.

"I'm sorry, you can put me down." She glanced to see the women watching from the doorways of their tents.

"No. I like carrying you." His long strides ate up the desert ground. Samir and Khalid were at the entrance to their tent.

"Everything is set up and security is watching," Khalid said.

"You need some sleep," Malik said to his brother.

"I will, but first Samir and I will trade off shifts guarding the entrance to your tent," Khalid said.

"Is that really necessary?" Catherine asked, looking at Khalid.

"Yes, it is," Malik said.

Khalid raised his eyebrows. "We want both of you to be safe. Enjoy your night." He pulled back the tent flap.

"Thank you, brother." Malik ducked inside.

Catherine's eyes widened. From the outside the tent didn't look like much, but inside ... "Amazing," she whispered.

Lanterns were hung from the sides of the tent. A low table was off to the right side, with colorful pillows around it. Off on the left side on a low platform was a bed with the most beautiful quilt covering it. It was black, with a gold, red, teal, and maroon design on each individual square.

"Please put me down," she said softly. Once she was on her feet, she wondered around the tent. "This is beautiful." She ran her hand over the quilt, its softness tickling her skin.

"All for you," Malik said, sweeping off his headdress before striding to her side and removing hers.

"Me?"

"Yes." He brushed her hair away from her face, and she shivered at the look of desire in his dark eyes. "I wanted you to be comfortable."

"I would be comfortable sleeping on the desert floor as long as I'm with you," she whispered. It was true.

Malik let out a groan. "If I make love to you, you will have to be quiet. The walls here are not exactly soundproof."

"I can be quiet." She ran her hand over his face, reveling in the slight roughness.

He lowered his head and their lips met in a kiss. When they broke apart, both were breathing hard. Malik turned from her and made his way around the tent, turning off the lanterns.

Her heart pounded. Maybe when everything settled down, she could convince Malik to bring her back out into the desert and make love to her under the stars. Her breath caught in her throat. No, she couldn't think that way. The engagement was fake. She couldn't fall for the fairytale. But for tonight she'd indulge herself a bit. Malik was a prince, after all.

The day after they returned from the desert, Catherine made her way to the family dining room. She'd left Lillianna fuming in her sitting room. She'd had enough of that woman. Catherine still had a few aches, but she wasn't sure if it was from the horse or falling off the mattress in the tent.

She stifled a giggle. She and Malik had gotten a little out of control, and she'd rolled right off the bed. Not that they'd been that far off the ground, but Malik had been concerned. She'd just laughed and told him she was fine.

Catherine was glad she'd had some time in the desert with Malik. The tribal leaders had been very open in discussing their issues, and before they left they told Malik they would talk to the other two leaders who had not been able to attend. However, they had no reason to oppose Malik's leadership.

She entered the dining room and her gaze landed on Jamal. A smile curved her lips; she strode over to Jamal. "It's great to see you home." She dropped a kiss on his cheek before taking her seat next to Malik. "Good morning, Anna."

"You're looking well this morning," Anna said, her eyes twinkling.

"Yes, the desert air agrees with me." Catherine poured a cup of coffee.

Malik glanced at her and winked before his features turned serious. "From now on, you'll have a personal security detail at all times."

Well, so much for easing back into real life. That lord-of-the-manor tone was back, and Catherine resented it. Dominance in the bedroom was one thing, outside was another. Turning her head, she gave him what she hoped was a pleasant smile. "No, thank you. I already have all the security I need."

"It's not up for discussion." She would stay calm, even if it killed her, and it just might. This man was able to bring out emotions she thought she'd buried years ago.

"You will have a security detail regardless of what you want." Malik scooped up some fruit from the bowl and placed it on her plate.

"Malik, dear——" started his mother.

"No, Mother. This I will not budge on. Catherine needs to be protected at all times."

Catherine bit her lower lip to stop from grinning. Anna was trying to diffuse the situation, and Catherine smiled at her in gratitude. She glanced at Jamal, who was trying to hide a smile behind his napkin. "If you'd stop being so bull-headed and listen, your mother is trying to diplomatically tell you to stop giving orders and try asking for a change."

Malik blinked several times, then glanced from Catherine to his mother and back again, a look of total bewilderment on his face.

Shaking her head, Catherine grinned. "Why, yes, Malik, thank you," she started. "Adding additional security would be nice. But let's keep it to two bulky males, please. I don't need a whole football team to take care of me. Oh, and if we could make them tall, dark, and extremely good-looking, I wouldn't mind at all."

Silence descended, then Malik burst out laughing. "Lord, woman, you'd drive a saint to drink."

"And you, sir, should have learned by now I don't take orders." She leaned over and whispered, "Unless we're in the bedroom." Heat flared in his eyes as she pulled back.

"I'm beginning to understand. Samir and two others I personally picked from my security force will now become yours."

"Won't you need them?"

He waved a hand. "These are men who are specially trained and report to me and no one else. You need to be protected until the man who assaulted you is captured." The irritation in his voice was clear.

"Judging by the noise he made when I head-butted him, I'd say he's got a broken nose and a couple of broken toes as well."

This time Jamal gave a hearty laugh. "Tell me, my dear, where did you learn to defend yourself so well?"

Catherine leaned back in her chair. It was time to come clean about a few things. "I learned before I was a teenager that if you can get away from a would-be kidnapper or assailant, do so. I had self-defense classes from the time I was ten until I turned sixteen."

"Why was that necessary?" Malik placed an arm over the back of her chair, his heat slipping into her skin.

She took a deep breath. "My parents are Baron and Baroness Hatcher." There, the first cat was out of the bag. Her parents were low on the royal totem pole, nowhere near the line of succession, but that never stopped them from flaunting the connection. Silence descended on the room, this time an oppressive one. Her heart dropped to her feet.

Malik curved his fingers around her shoulder and squeezed.

Taking a deep breath, she began to speak. "The headline Malik showed me, where my parents were quoted saying that I had betrayed them, would be accurate from their point of view."

"A flawed point of view," Malik said.

His words, and his taking her side before knowing all the

facts, warmed her heart, giving her the courage to continue. "From the time I was a small child until I left home at eighteen, my parents decided the best way to keep themselves in the news was to keep me in front of the press." Out of the corner of her eye she caught Malik's wince. Reaching up, she covered his hand, which still rested on her shoulder. "Your reasons were valid, theirs were simple selfishness."

"I thank you for that," Malik said.

Catherine blew out a breath. "The press ate it up, and I became the center of attention. I hated it."

"Well, of course you did," Anna said. "No child wants that kind of attention."

"That was the reason we protected our sons during their childhood and teenage years from the paparazzi," Jamal said.

Catherine was surprised at how easily the words flowed. The unconditional understanding from Malik and his parents caused her heart to lighten and helped her realize this family meant more to her than her own. "I couldn't move without the paparazzi being there. Eventually I stopped going out, and I spent more and more of my time in my room studying or reading. That's how I found my love for drawing."

"It couldn't have been easy for you growing up in that environment," Malik said.

"No. As a child I wasn't able to defy my parents, but as a teenager, they found it harder and harder to force me into situations I didn't want to be in." Her stomach cramped at the memories of being paraded in front of the press, dressed up like a doll to be shown off.

Malik took her hand, raised it to his lips, and gently kissed her knuckles. "I'm sorry I put you in a position that reminded you of your dreadful childhood."

Her lips turned up in a half smile. "Your reasons were sound. You're working toward helping your country and people. You're not narcissistic, like my parents."

"You forgive me?" His dark eyes were filled with hope.

"I forgave you a long time ago for what happened when we first met. Sometimes events get out of control, and all we can do is go with the flow." A sense of peace overcame her. Her words were true; she'd forgiven Malik, and none of what was currently happening was his fault.

"Wise words from a very young, but intelligent, woman," Jamal said.

Catherine nodded and continued with her story; better to get it out now. "I left home at eighteen and began to study art. My parents were horrified their daughter would do such a thing. They wanted me to follow in my mother's footsteps—marry a rich man, be a wife and mother. Not to have dreams or to study art or to have my own mind." She let out a breath, and her muscles began to relax. "They milked the press with the story for over a year before they realized I wasn't going to respond."

How much more should she explain? Her heart skipped a beat as she glanced around the table. Here was the caring, compassionate family she had wanted growing up, and now she had it. They had a right to know, but she wasn't sure if she could tell them everything. She didn't want to see pity in their eyes.

"When I was twenty, I met Jamie Monroe." The room swam as her vision blurred. "He was a musician. A very talented musician."

"I remember reading an article about him not too long ago," Anna said. "He passed away several years or so ago. Cancer, I believe."

"Yes." Catherine bit her lower lip and forced herself to continue. "He couldn't handle the press and all the attention. All he wanted to do was play guitar, sing, and make people happy with his music. The pressure from the press helped in killing him."

The king and queen nodded, and Catherine was surprised at how well they were taking this. She risked peeking at Malik from beneath her lashes. Instead of the pity and shock she expected to see, she saw concern in those dark eyes, and a gleam of respect and understanding.

"You're all taking this very well, and I have to wonder why." They were calm, very calm. Then it dawned on her. "You had me investigated." Why hadn't she thought about that before?

"Standard procedure when someone comes to live in the royal household," Jamal said.

Catherine glanced at Malik. He shook his head. "I only saw the names of your parents and some highlights. I never read the full report," Malik said.

The room went silent. Catherine was tired of this dark cloud over them. Jamal and Anna were within their rights to have her checked out before she arrived. And if they didn't have issues with her parents, she could let it go. "Well, since you know where I come from, can we please dump the protocol barracuda?"

Laughter filled the room, and for the first time in a long time the darkness plaguing her was gone, allowing the light to shine through. Maybe, just maybe, everything would be okay.

"I think I can arrange that," Malik said. "But you need to go shopping for clothes. We've got a state dinner and an engagement party to attend."

"State dinner?" She dropped the croissant she was about to take a bite of onto the plate.

"Yes. It's on your schedule. While my parents will be there, it is important for you and me to show a united front," Malik said.

"Great," she muttered. Shopping and a room full of dignitaries.

"More than great," Malik whispered in her ear. "Now I have an excuse to hold you in my arms."

A shiver swept through Catherine's body as she filled with warmth and desire.

Catherine paced around her room. Her maid had left after helping her dress. Now, there was nothing to do but wait for Malik.

The gown Anna insisted she wear, if you could call the garment that, fell in soft whispers around her ankles. It wasn't one of those low-cut, daring outfits, but Catherine was still apprehensive.

She wore nothing underneath the silky fabric but a pair of minuscule panties. The maid insisted no slip or other undergarments were necessary. The gown itself was beautiful, with sparkling red and gold embellishments sewn into the fabric.

Forcing herself to keep her hands at her sides so as not to mess up her hair, she continued to pace and went over everything Anna had told her about who would be at the dinner.

A knock sounded and she jumped. Putting her hands on her stomach, she took a deep breath, then moved across the room and opened the door.

Malik's jaw dropped open.

"I told Anna this was wrong." Catherine stepped back, ready to close the door.

"No," he croaked out, putting his hand on the door and moving into the room. He cleared his throat. "For me to tell you that you look beautiful is an understatement. You take my breath away." He captured her hands in his. "Your hands are freezing."

"I'm nervous." Her voice was shaky. Damn, why had she agreed to this? All she really wanted to do was curl up in bed and hide.

"How can I help you?"

She almost said by letting her not go to the party, but she couldn't. "I'll be okay."

"Will you?" He cupped her cheek with his palm. Hot tendrils of sensation flowed through her veins. "It's okay to be nervous. I'll be by your side all night."

"But this gown." She gestured with her hand, and he took a step back. "I feel so exposed."

"You pay me, and our people, a great honor by wearing the royal colors. No one will doubt you are my chosen bride."

Heat flared in her cheeks. His chosen bride, she really wished she could believe that. This was all because her parents were narcissistic idiots and the tabloids loved a good, juicy story.

"Shall we go down?"

"If I say no, can we stay here?" There was a hopeful tone in her voice.

"As much as I'd like nothing better than to spend the evening with you in my bed and us exploring more of your limits, I'm afraid not."

She sighed as her cheeks grew warmer. "I guess I'm as ready as I'll ever be."

"You'll do fine." He pulled her hand through his arm. His support meant so much to her. "They're going to love you."

She hoped so, because even if their engagement was fake, he needed the support of his people.

"You were the hit of the dinner," Malik said, holding Catherine to his side as the last guest left.

"Maybe." She leaned against him. The state dinner hadn't been the ordeal she'd thought it was going to be.

All the guests accepted her place at Malik's side, and she found all of them very open to a woman who was intelligent. Not one man condescended to her. Well, there was one. Malik's minister of information watched her like a hawk all evening, as if he were afraid she'd run off with the royal silver or something. But all in all, she'd had a wonderful time, especially when Jamal danced with her on the dance floor. While he admitted to being tired, he told her she was a bright spot in his life.

Catherine was falling more and more in love with Malik and his family. They so readily accepted her for who she was, something that didn't happen very often. Joy and happiness flowed through her.

"Tired?" Malik asked as he tightened his arms around her waist.

"A little." Tonight, she'd learned more about him and his work with the tribal leaders, his attempts to bring them together, and his work with the villages on the edges of town, to make sure they were involved. Plus, he was passionate about making sure all children were healthy and educated. She was falling hard for this caring, compassionate, sexy, and dominant man.

No matter how many times she reminded herself it wasn't a good idea to fall for him, her heart and body didn't care. After saying their good nights to the family, they walked up the stairs to their rooms. Where they would normally turn right to her room, Malik maneuvered her left. Outside the door to his room, he lifted his hands and his palms framed her face. "Stay the night with me."

Catherine's heart stuttered. They'd played together before this, but other than when she was attacked and their night in the desert, she'd never spent the entire night in his room, always leaving before morning. She nodded and

Malik grinned. Releasing her, he took her hand, opened the door, and tugged her inside.

The door slid shut, and he pulled her into his arms. "Alone at last." He lowered his head, and his lips covered hers.

Catherine melted into his embrace. She so wanted to be with him, she shoved away her doubts about being found in his room in the morning, about her role, about everything. Only Malik mattered.

Their tongues tangled. His kisses were like a drug she couldn't get enough of. And it seemed he couldn't, either. When they parted, both were breathing heavily.

"I want you so much," he whispered.

"I want you too."

He captured her mouth once again, and his hands slid down her body, gathering up the material of her gown. He broke this kiss only to whisk the caftan over her head.

A wave of shyness came over her, and she raised her hands to cover herself.

"No." He captured her hands in his. "I want to look at you."

"Malik." She squirmed beneath his gaze. He'd seen her naked before, but for some reason this time was different. Hotter, more erotic than anything she'd experienced with him.

"You are truly breathtaking." He kissed his way to the curve of her neck.

The passion blazing in his eyes melted Catherine's nervousness. She trusted him to give into the pleasure he created in her. He trailed his lips down her body, awaking nerves she didn't know existed. She slid her fingers through his dark hair, enjoying its silky texture. "One of us is overdressed."

He lifted his head, a wicked grin forming. "I wonder who that could be." He slipped his finger beneath her panties and stripped them off.

Her knees went weak as he knelt at her feet gazing up at her nude body. "Not fair," she whispered.

"All's fair in my world." He rose and removed his caftan, then his briefs, and tossed them both aside.

Oh, dear Lord. She swallowed. He was magnificent. His skin glowed with desire, and his penis was erect. Very erect. Catherine took a deep breath as Malik lifted her into his arms and then sat her on the bed.

He knelt beside her on the mattress. "Such pretty pink nipples." His lips closed over her left nipple. Licking, sucking, nipping, before doing the same to the right.

Electric shocks shot from her nipples to her core with each tug of his mouth. His fingers closed around her wrists and lifted her arms above her head. "Will you leave them there, or do I have to restrain you?" he asked.

Oh, Lord, what was he going to do? "I'll keep them above my head."

With a nod, he released her wrists and trailed his lips from her breasts to her stomach. His hot breath caressed her skin. He placed his palms on the inside of her thighs. "Open."

She shifted on the bed and opened her legs. He knelt between them, leaning down to blow on her pussy. Her muscles tightened as he slid his fingers to her nether lips and held them open.

Unable to help herself, she squirmed on the mattress. "Be still." His tone was firm.

"You're killing me."

"Not yet I'm not."

Before she could react, he dipped his head and licked her pussy. Her muscles tightened, and her stomach contracted as she fought not to move while he licked and nipped at her clit.

His fingers danced along the outside of her thighs before moving inward. Somehow she kept still as he slid two fingers into her.

"So wet," he said, raising his head to stare at her.

"Only for you." And it was true. It hit her right then, she was in love with Malik. She trusted him more than she trusted any other man, with her body, her soul, her heart.

"Mine." He drew his fingers back and then plunged them back into her.

Her back arched as his fingers curved inside her, finding that special spot. Tremors shook her body. "I'm going to come if you keep doing that."

He grinned. "Can't have that." He removed his fingers from her core and reached over to the nightstand. The drawer rattled, then he sat back on his heels with a condom between his fingers. Malik ripped the foil and rolled the condom down his cock.

"All mine," he whispered. He rose over her and guided himself into her pussy.

Hard and needy was all she could think as he pushed past her entrance.

"You're tight," he whispered, his lips next to her ear.

"It's been a while since I've had sex."

He gazed at her, and she swore his cock grew bigger at her words. "I'll go slow."

"No." She flexed her hips and he stilled. Oh, heck, she wasn't supposed to make demands in the bedroom. "Ummm, sorry."

"You're forgiven." He shifted his hips, pushing into her. Her inner muscles stretched around him. Her skin tingled.

"You feel so good, so hard, so hot." She fisted her hands so as not to touch him as he pushed all the way into her. She let out a moan. So full. On instinct, she tightened her core muscles.

Malik groaned. "So fucking snug." He backed out and then thrust forward.

"Oh, yes." Her arms shook with the need to touch him, but she'd promised to keep her hands over her head.

In and out. Her neck arched as he picked up the pace. "Please, harder, faster." Her breathing increased as the pleasure soared through her veins. Nerves tingled with delight.

"I want to make this good for you."

"You are. I'm ready to shatter into a thousand pieces." Her inner muscles clasped him with every stroke. God, he seemed to swell even bigger inside her. She raised her hips to meet his with each thrust.

His mouth covered hers as a fluttering sensation started in her belly, then spread quickly. She wasn't going to last. She tore her mouth from his and cried out as her orgasm overwhelmed her.

Their gazes locked. Malik's eyes filled with desire and need. He continued to thrust into her willing body. Each stroke took her higher and higher. Her body shook with the force of her second climax. Then he stiffened and pulsed inside her as his own release took over.

Malik collapsed against her, laying his head on her shoulder. Catherine smiled, enjoying his weight on her body. She lowered her arms and stroked his sweaty back. Her body hummed with satisfaction.

He licked her neck and flexed his hips.

"Again," she whispered.

"Anything you say, my princess."

An hour later, Catherine snuggled against Malik's warm body, her body not only sated, but deliciously sore. She was one lucky woman. Half-asleep, she wiggled again, finding that sweet spot, when Malik kissed the top of her head and whispered, "I can't wait to make you my wife."

Her heart tightened. Too bad it was pillow talk.

Catherine woke the next morning alone. Wait a second. Her eyes focused on the chair next to the bed. She was back in her room. Sitting up, she turned and saw a single rose lying on the pillow next to her. A smile curved her lips as she picked up the flower and brought it to her nose.

The deep rich fragrance filled her. Stretching, she climbed out of bed. Muscles protested. Malik must have carried her back to her room early this morning so no one would talk about their spending the night together. Private, special words nudged at her memory, but escaped her when she tried to focus on them.

Hugging her arms around her stomach, she practically danced into the bathroom. She wasn't sorry she'd made love to Malik again. No, it had been a liberating and exciting night. She missed his arms around her already.

Whoa, girl, don't get in too deep, she thought. Oh, who was she kidding, she was already too deep. She was totally and completely in love with Malik. A few weeks ago, the thought would have had her running for the hills, now … she stared at herself in the mirror. She didn't look different, but she felt different. Her world was brighter and happier.

With a goofy grin, she pushed aside her fanciful thoughts, took a quick shower, dressed, and went downstairs for breakfast. She was surprised to see the only person in the room was Malik.

"Good morning," he said, rising when she walked in.

"Good morning." Before she could take another step, he was in front of her, pulling her into his arms and kissing her. In the back of her mind, she realized that anyone could walk in on them, but the texture of his lips against hers, her tongue dueling with his, made her forget everything else.

Malik lifted his head and stared down at her. "That's how I want to start every morning."

Her face grew warm. "It is good, isn't it?" She danced out of his embrace, sat down, and dished up breakfast.

"We've got about fifteen minutes before we need to be in my father's office." He took a seat beside her.

Her appetite fled at his announcement. "Is there something wrong?"

"No, my dove." He ran his fingers over her cheek. "He

would like a meeting with us to discuss the next step in our country."

"But shouldn't that be decided by family?"

"You are family. You are my fiancée, and therefore you will be involved."

But she really wasn't. This was a fake engagement, after all. "Okay." Catherine shrugged her shoulders, but she had a feeling that not only agreeing to allow the family to announce her and Malik's engagement, but her presence was helping keep the pretense up. She'd have to leave once her job was completed, and then what? She glanced at Malik. Yes, she loved him, but marrying him was a fantasy; she wasn't royal material.

"I'm stepping down, and Malik will become the new king of Bashir," Jamal announced.

Catherine's stomach knotted. The end had come sooner than she expected. Malik would become the ruler, and as soon as she finished the mural, she would be leaving.

"According to tradition, once I make the formal announcement to our people, Malik will take the throne in two weeks."

Her gaze drifted over to Malik. He sat there straight-faced, no emotions showing. He was a man born to lead, whereas she was a woman born to heartbreak. Unable to sit any longer, she rose to her feet. "I need to get to the hospital." The mural needed her attention if she was going to be done in the next two weeks. Then she could go home. Her heart skipped a beat. Home. She wasn't sure where that was anymore.

"I'll go with you." Malik stood.

"I'm sure you have other things you need to talk with your father about." There she was, running away again. When would she break the habit?

"Nothing that can't wait." He cupped her elbow. "Until later, Father." Malik escorted her from the room. Once they were in the hallway, he swung her to face him. "You don't look happy at the announcement."

"My happiness doesn't matter." It didn't. She disliked that she could be hurting him, but she didn't have a choice. She couldn't stay.

"Yes, it does." He took her hand and led her down the hall and into his office, then leaned against the door after he shut it. "What is wrong?"

"Nothing." Catherine wrapped her arms around her waist and stared at the gold carpet.

"Catherine." His soft, gentle fingers touched her chin. "Look at me."

"This is going to change your life, Malik." She kept her gaze on the floor.

"Not just my life," he whispered as he slid his arms around her, trapping her arms between his body and hers.

She tried to shake her head, but his lips kissed their way down from her ear to her neck.

"Everything will be okay. I'll be with you every step of the way."

A shiver worked its way up from her toes as his lips continued kissing their way down her neck and then back up to her chin, to her cheek, and then her temple. "Malik." She lifted her head. If only she could get over her need of him.

"Better." He framed her face with his hands. "I promised you I'd never leave you alone to face this, and I'm going to keep that promise." He kissed her softly.

Unable to help herself, she kissed him back, wanting to be with him more than she wanted anything in her life. So instead of fighting him, she'd savor every second she had with him now, because soon she'd be alone again.

Malik led Catherine to the waiting car. His father's announcement hadn't been a shock. They'd discussed it already. It was time. His father had explained he wanted to step down and spend more time with his wife, Malik's mother. Malik approved. He glanced over at Catherine as the vehicle started moving. Worry clouded her blue eyes. He wasn't sure what she was worried about. "So, tell me. How much longer will it be before the mural is done?" Maybe if he talked to her about her work, she'd relax.

"Less than two weeks."

"The kids are very excited."

"So am I. I can't wait to see their faces when they see the mural completed. They've inspired so much of it." She smiled, and Malik was pleased to see the worry flee from her eyes as they talked about her work.

But he kept an eye on Catherine when they arrived at the hospital. The attack last week still bothered him, and the culprit hadn't been caught. He was going to accompany her to speak to a little girl and her family across the parking lot, but Catherine told him to stay put. Now, she laughed at something the little girl had said. She ruffled the child's hair, and said something to the parents, then turned back to him.

His gut tightened as she sauntered across the pavement. This woman took his breath away like no other. And he wasn't going to let her go.

The shouts of the guards were his first indication something was wrong. He glanced over his shoulder in time to see a black car speeding their way. And Catherine was right in its path, frozen in place.

Finally she turned, Malik grabbed her arm, and together they ran, then he pushed them both through the doors.

Metal scraped against metal. Glass shattered, and cries were all he heard for the next few moments. It wasn't until he blinked several times that he saw the smoke and dust in the air. Malik could barely breathe. They were safe, at least for the moment.

"Malik?" She touched his head, and a fine layer of concrete dust floated from his hair.

"I'm okay." He rolled to his feet, and pulled her up and into his arms. "Are you hurt?"

"No." She tightened her arms around him, then a shudder swept through her body as her knees buckled.

Malik turned and saw the car embedded in the doorway. If he hadn't grabbed her arm and flung them both into the hospital … "I thought for a moment … " He buried his hands in her hair.

"I was startled, and it took me a second or two to react. I'm sorry if I scared you." Her heart beat against his.

"Scared is a mild word for what I was feeling." He tilted her head and looked into her eyes. "Never, ever, scare me like that again." He lowered his mouth to hers and captured her lips in a hard, brief kiss.

"Your Highness," Samir interrupted.

Not about to let Catherine go, Malik tucked her against his body. "Was there anyone in the car?"

"No. Remote controlled."

"Find him." Samir nodded. What the hell was going on? This was the second attempt on Catherine's life. Who was behind this? The tribal leaders? He didn't think so. Once maybe, but not twice, and they were more direct than using a vehicle.

"What the hell happened?" Hassan ran over to the pair. "We've got alarms going off all over the place. Is anyone hurt?"

"We're fine." Malik glanced at the wreckage, then at his brother.

"Is it always this exciting here?" Catherine asked.

Both men stared at her, then Malik smiled, and Hassan gave a small laugh.

"Crazy woman," muttered Hassan.

"Does nothing faze you?" asked Malik.

"I made you smile, didn't I?" She grinned at him, but her face turned somber as she glanced over his shoulder.

The press had gathered and were taking pictures when the local police arrived.

"Let's go someplace less public." He guided her away from the wreckage. This was no accident.

"I need to work." Catherine told Malik, for what seemed like the hundredth time. The police had taken their statements, the car had been towed away, and not even two hours later there was a team of construction workers fixing the mess. But he couldn't let her go.

"I'd rather you come back to the palace with me." At least there she'd be safe. Leaving her at the hospital went against every nerve in his body.

"No. I know you're worried." She placed her palm against his cheek. He savored her soft skin against his. "Work will help me settle down."

"You could have been killed." He had to get back to the palace and discuss this latest attempt on her life, but he couldn't stop thinking about the car. What would have happened if the car had arrived a few minutes earlier? Or later? How many people might have been hurt or killed? The "what ifs" kept running through his mind.

"But I wasn't. And it could have been you they were aiming at."

He shook his head. "It was you. You were right in the path, if I hadn't grabbed your arm and we both made a mad dash … " He didn't want to scare her any more than she already was. "Just promise me you won't leave the hospital until I come back, and no ditching your bodyguards."

"I promise." She tilted her head and stared up at him.

He puffed out a breath at the earnest look in her eyes. "All right." He dipped his head. "Behave or I'll spank you."

"That gives me a reason to be naughty."

"Not if I spank you with a nice hard wooden paddle."

"Yes, sir. I'll be good." She shivered in his arms.

He wasn't sure if the shiver was anticipation or apprehension, but both were good. "Minx." He dropped a kiss on her lips.

She flashed him a grin before he strode away.

24

The next week passed in a blur. Malik settled down at his desk for the day. Four days ago, his father had announced to the country he was stepping down. And since then, Malik's life had become a whirlwind of activity. Not that it hadn't been before, but now it was much worse. The only saving grace was Catherine. When she was by his side, he didn't feel the pressure of what being king would mean. She was his calming force.

As busy as he was, she made sure he sat down and relaxed after dinner. A smile crept over his lips. The first night she'd drawn him into her room and pushed him down onto the sofa, his blood heated. Then she began to ask him about his day.

At the time, he hadn't realized how important it was for him to discuss his day with her. It allowed him to decompress, but also allowed him to discuss his worries. Catherine never judged, and the woman was damn intelligent. She'd offer comments and suggestions. She even defended Omar when Malik wasn't happy with his minister.

A knock at his door had him raising his head, and he was surprised to see his brother Khalid poke his head around the open frame. "I need you to come to the public chamber."

Malik rose to his feet. "What is it?"

"We found the man we think is responsible for the attacks on Catherine."

"Well, Ahmed?" said Malik, staring at the man who'd tried to hurt Catherine. As much as he wanted to choke the life out of Ahmed, he couldn't. As the future ruler, he had to hide his emotions and follow the law, but that didn't mean he wasn't tempted.

"Please, Your Highness, I only meant to frighten the woman."

"Why?"

Ahmed flinched at the question. "Because the person I worked for wanted her to leave the country. He says she doesn't belong. He is impatient. His last order to me was to get rid of her, but I couldn't."

Malik froze in place. Someone wanted Catherine dead. No. That was not going to happen, not now, not ever—well, not until they were both very, very old. He protected what was his, and she was his. "Who ordered you to do this? And what did you hope to gain?" Pacing helped him keep his anger under control, but it would only work for so long.

The man bowed his head. "Money. I needed the money, Your Highness."

The man's voice trembled, but a note of shame was there as well. Malik hesitated, suspecting something wasn't right. "Why did you need the money?" He gentled his tone.

"My wife is ill, Your Highness. Her illness requires medication I can't afford. I was told if I scared your girl-friend away, I would be given all I needed." The man openly wept as he sank to his knees. "I swear to you, Your Highness, I would never hurt your woman. I could not."

"Easy." Malik knelt next to the man. As much as he and his father were trying to do for their people, some of them were still not getting the help they needed. He cupped the man's shoulder. "I need to know who paid you."

The man swallowed. "I fear, not for my life, but that of my wife."

"Do not fear." He looked up at his brother, who nodded. "As soon as you tell me who hired you, Khalid will take you to your wife and transport you both to the hospital, where your wife will be taken care of without charge."

Ahmed nodded. "It was Omar—"

Malik rose to his feet and started out of the room even before Ahmed finished saying the name.

"Malik!" Khalid yelled.

He didn't stop. Fury like he'd never experienced before coursed through his veins. How dare Omar try to hurt Catherine! Malik walked rapidly down the hall, looking in offices until he found his minister of information in his father's office.

"Malik, there you are," said his father. "Omar was just—"

"You bastard." Malik grabbed Omar by the collar and pressed him up against the wall. "Did you really think you could get away with it?"

Not only was Malik's anger directed at his minister of information, but it was also at himself. He'd let this man get close to Catherine, ignored his put-downs and his protests. If only he'd paid more attention.

"Your …Your Highness," Omar stuttered.

"Malik, what are you doing?" His father was on his feet.

Malik started to answer when the minister's eyes widened, a hint of fear entering them, as he glanced over Malik's shoulder. Then, in an instant, coldness replaced the fear. Malik turned his head to see his brother and Ahmed standing in the office doorway.

Without releasing the minister, Malik spoke. "Omar hired Ahmed to frighten Catherine into leaving the country, and when that didn't work, he told Ahmed to kill Catherine."

"That's ridiculous," the minister said.

"You deny it?" Malik tightened his hold. "Are you not the one who kept suggesting I keep my distance from

Catherine? Not spend time with her, even after our engagement was announced? The one who criticized her at every step?" Anger flowed through Malik's veins.

"Enough," his father said. "Let go of the minister, and let's get this straightened out."

His father's hard tone and order had Malik gritting his teeth. "Watch yourself, Omar. I'm not as forgiving as my father," Malik whispered before releasing the man and stepping back.

"I'm sure this is a simple misunderstanding." The minister straightened his clothing.

"Is this the man who paid you?" Malik asked Ahmed.

"Yes, Your Highness."

"He is lying." Omar's hands clenched at his sides, but his eyes were hard and dead.

"I have no reason to lie." Ahmed spread his hands out in front of him. "You promised me that my wife would be taken care of. Instead, she is still lying in our small home, without the medicine she needs, because you refused to pay me."

Omar drew himself up and stared at Ahmed. "You are nothing."

The contempt in Omar's voice almost caused Malik to hit him. His minister was lying through his teeth. His body language was tense and defensive. And Malik had an idea of how to prove the man was lying.

"Khalid, please take Ahmed to my office." Ahmed

opened his mouth. Malik leaned over. "Easy, my friend," he whispered. "Trust me to fix this situation."

Ahmed bowed his head.

Malik turned to his father. "Father, please keep my minister here while I check out some facts."

"I have work to do," the minister blustered, moving toward the door.

Two guards blocked him.

"For now, you will wait here," his father announced.

Malik inclined his head to his father and left the room. An hour later, he walked back into his father's office with all the proof he needed.

Catherine stepped back and smiled. The mural was done. She turned in a slow circle, taking in each wall. The walls were filled with animals and plants, most of them native to Bashir.

Thanks to Hassan, she was able to create flowering plants and flowers from where the medical equipment would be attached to the walls. The sense of accomplishment warmed her heart, but at the same time her heart broke. She no longer had a reason to stay in Bashir.

"This is incredible."

Catherine turned to see the queen standing in the doorway. "I'm happy you like it."

"The children will love it. You've done a magnificent job."

Catherine gathered her materials together. "What brings you here?"

"I was hoping to convince you to take a break and have tea with me, but since you're done, we can return home for our tea."

"That would be nice."

Samir and two other bodyguards were waiting outside the door. They escorted Catherine and the queen to the waiting car. They had barely cleared the outside hospital door when the press descended.

"Is it true?" one yelled.

"How do you feel about having your past revealed?" another yelled.

More bodyguards surrounded them as Catherine and Anna made their way to the car. Camera flashes blinded them. What were they talking about?

"Is the prince still going to marry you, knowing you caused the death of Jamie Monroe?"

The question brought Catherine up short. One of the press corps members shoved a newspaper into her hand.

"Catherine." Anna urged her into the waiting car.

Catherine clutched the paper in her fist as she climbed in, fear filling her heart.

Her fear was realized the moment she looked down at the front page. "Prince Malik's future wife implicated in the death of Jamie Monroe."

"It's trash," Anna said.

"Only if you don't believe it," whispered Catherine, closing her eyes. She didn't want to see the pity in the queen's gaze.

When they reached the palace, Catherine turned to Anna. "Excuse me for not having tea with you, but I'm not feeling well." Without waiting for an answer, Catherine wearily climbed the stairs. Once inside her room, she began to read the paper.

Her stomach churned and tumbled as she relived every minute of the night Jamie died. The night she could no longer keep her silence about. She'd failed Jamie as a friend and pretend lover. The night he died, she'd struck out at the press for their intrusion, but it had stopped them from knowing Jamie chose to die that night. A shiver swept through her body.

She couldn't handle reporters and she'd never be able to. She had to leave. Now. She wouldn't let Malik's name and family be drawn into her mess.

After pulling her suitcase from the closet, she packed. If Malik realized what she was doing, he wouldn't let her leave. He would try to protect her, and in doing so, ruin his good name. She refused to let that happen. He was destined to be king. And she was destined to be alone.

25

Malik prowled around the room. He wanted to go to Catherine, but she had called him and told him she needed some time alone. He had to respect her request.

His mother told him how the press had descended on them and about the newspaper Catherine had seen. He hadn't known the depth of his minister's hatred until that moment.

How could he explain that one of his most trusted advisors had fed the story to the press, knowing what it would do? Let alone, that same advisor was responsible for all the accidents? Would she understand he didn't care what the story said? Would she believe him when he told her he loved her?

He stopped pacing. He loved her. The words turned

over in his mind. "You are an idiot," he whispered in the empty room.

He didn't care about her past. He cared about her and how the past affected her, but it couldn't touch him or his love for her.

He'd read the story himself and could see exactly why she refused to see him and hid in her room. Plus, it had given him insight as to why she hated the paparazzi so much. His life was filled with them. He worried about Catherine being able to cope with that.

But so far she'd done a wonderful job of dealing with them. Yes, he decided, she would be able to handle herself and anything they threw at her once she believed in his love. He longed to go to her, to take her into his arms and tell her how much he loved her. They could weather this storm together. But her request to be left alone held him back.

Time. He had to give her time.

After a restless night and a morning of waiting, Malik knocked on Catherine's door. It was after ten. She didn't usually sleep this late, but after yesterday he couldn't blame her. "Catherine," he called, and knocked again. Still no response. He twisted the knob and walked in.

The silence was so complete his muscles tightened and his stomach turned over. She wasn't in the room, his instincts told him that, but there was something else. The room was different, as if all the sunshine were gone.

He strode into the bedroom. Her bed was neatly made and there were two white envelopes sitting primly against the multicolored pillows. Crossing to the bed, he glanced at the closet. Her clothes were missing. All that hung there were the caftans in royal colors.

Heart pounding, Malik snatched up the envelope with his name on it and ripped it open.

Malik,

I hope you'll forgive me for what I've done. I never meant for any of this to happen. I hope all goes well for you and your family. You will make a perfect king.

Love,

Catherine

The word *love* gave him hope. Anger flared deep within his gut. At her for leaving, at the paparazzi, and at himself for not anticipating her need to run. Well, he wasn't going to let her go. There was nowhere she could hide from him.

He picked up the second envelope and marched out of the room. Yelling for Samir, he ran down the stairs. If anyone knew where Catherine had gone, it would be Samir.

Malik had to move quickly. Somehow, Catherine had managed to circumvent his security force yet again and made her way out of the palace without a bodyguard and, he suspected, a driver.

Heads would roll, but not until he found Catherine and

brought her back. But that meant sitting everyone down and all of them being on the same page.

Catherine sat in the airport lounge nursing a cup of strong Arabic coffee. She'd exploited the security flaw in the garden again and stopped at the hospital to say a silent goodbye before taking a taxi to the airport. She'd sat next to Zain's bed with tears in her eyes. She was going to miss the little boy. She'd written him a note and left it with the small stuffed elephant in the chair for him to find when he woke.

In the taxi, she'd called her best friend, Sara, and asked her to meet her at the airport with the promise to fill her in once she got home. She didn't want to discuss it in a taxi where the driver could overhear.

Catherine glanced up at the TV blaring in the corner of the room. The news confirmed the preparations for Malik's coronation were almost complete. She'd forgotten with everything else going on the coronation was just four days away. How would Malik cope?

Her heart stuttered. Malik hid his emotions in public, but in private with her, he'd finally let his guard down. She'd encouraged him when they spent time alone at night to talk to her about anything and everything. Bottling up emotions could cause major problems, she was well aware of that. Jamie had been a classic case.

She sighed. Hopefully, by the time of the coronation, the

story of her and Jamie would be old news, and the press would leave Malik and his family alone. Out of the corner of her eye, Catherine noticed an elderly woman staring at her. She should be used to it. After everything, she was no longer a nonentity, but instead the prince's disgraced woman.

Turning her head, she smiled at the woman. "Good morning," she said, trying to be cheerful.

The woman smiled back. "Forgive me for staring, but I couldn't help it."

"It's all right." Catherine sipped her coffee, then a shadow fell over her, diverting her attention from the stranger.

"I had hoped I was wrong," a female voice said.

"Anna." Catherine jumped to her feet, spilling coffee over her hand. "Is Malik with you?"

"No." Her voice was stern and her jaw clenched as she stood stiffly staring at Catherine.

"I see." Catherine's heart squeezed, making it difficult to breathe. Anna was upset with her, and she'd never see Malik again once she boarded her plane. This time her heart wouldn't heal as it had after Jamie's death. There would always be a piece of it in Bashir with Malik.

"I don't think you do. Come with me, Catherine, and let's have a private talk." Anna's tone was commanding.

Catherine tried to find a way to decline, but one look at Anna's face had her changing her mind. Maybe she could explain why she'd left a note rather than saying goodbye in person. Guilt ate at her stomach. After picking up her bag, she followed Anna into a private room where Samir waited.

"Catherine," Anna started the moment they were seated.

"I'm sorry I left like I did. I didn't have a choice." The words rushed out of Catherine's mouth.

"You do have a choice. Either you love my son, or you don't." Anna's expression didn't soften. Mama bear was not happy that her son was being rejected.

Catherine sighed, because she wasn't rejecting Malik, the man; she was rejecting Malik, the king. Her heart squeezed tight. "I'm not the right woman for him."

Anna reached over and clasped Catherine's hands. "My son is a good man, an honorable man, but only a man. Whatever argument you may have had with him, please do not leave in anger. He will make a good king, and he needs a strong woman by his side. You are that woman."

"I'm not." The words pierced her heart like a dagger. "I'm obviously not strong enough since I'm being judged on past events. And the engagement was a ruse."

"Posh." The queen waved a hand in the air. "What do these crazy paparazzi know? You are a good woman—a woman who respects her adoptive country. What ruse?"

"The engagement? When it was first proposed it was all pretend, everyone understood that. But I'm no longer an asset, and going through with a wedding is too far to carry a pretense."

"I don't know what games you and my son played with

yourselves, but the engagement was real. That's why when you first said no, I agreed with you. No woman should be pushed into anything she doesn't want to do." Anna paused and patted Catherine's hand. "But when you stepped out on the balcony with the royal colors on, I knew you were a willing participant. What I see between you and my son is love."

"You can't know that."

"I do." She touched Catherine's cheek with a soft finger. "Look deep in your heart, my dear, and you'll know it too. You've been in the spotlight since you arrived in our country, and that would wear on anyone's nerves. You've handled yourself with grace, dignity, and the people respect you for it. You *should be* our crown princess."

"But … " Memories filtered through her brain. The zoo, the marketplace, the hospital, formal dinners. The people of Bashir smiling at her, calling out greetings, telling her how much they enjoyed seeing her with their crown prince. How they shooed the paparazzi away when they could or simply created a barrier so she could shop in private.

Even when the paparazzi caught her unaware, she didn't blow up at them or make any statements. She had done her best to keep her head held high and keep moving. Was Anna right?

"There are two sides to every story, and maybe it's time you told your side of it. Let the world see the compassionate woman I know is inside." The queen stood. "It is your choice, but know this, you have the support of the entire royal family." Then she walked out of the room, with Samir following.

Catherine sat there, stunned. Could what Anna said be true? For the first time, she saw her life in a different light. Maybe it was time she told her side of the story of her life and assumed her rightful place beside the man she loved, instead of running away. If Malik truly wanted her to be his wife, that is. If not, then she'd face reality and not be left wondering for the rest of her life. Taking a deep breath, she straightened her shoulders and stood.

Time to take charge of her life.

Striding into the airport lounge, she glanced around the room. It was almost full, and while people looked at her, there were none of the sly glances or whispering she'd endured after Jamie's death. There were two sides to every story. But could she do this? She tightened her fingers around her purse and walked out the door.

Samir stepped to her side, reaching for her luggage.

"Samir." She allowed him to take her bags from her.

"Where do we go, Miss Taylor?"

She let out a breath, grateful for Samir's presence. Anna must have ordered him to stay behind. "I need time to think. Can you find me a hotel where no one will look for me? And I need you to keep quiet about my whereabouts, no one must know I'm still here."

"Of course, Miss Taylor. The queen indicated I should do whatever you asked."

She followed Samir through a maze of doors until he led

her to a waiting vehicle. Catherine sent off a quick text to Sara, letting her know she wouldn't be on the airplane and she'd explain later. She had three days before Malik's pre-coronation party. Three days to figure her life out. Three days to sink or swim.

26

Malik stared out his bedroom window. How he longed to take his horse out and lose himself in the desert, but he couldn't. Tonight was his coronation party. Tomorrow he would be king.

For three days, his security forces had combed the airports, railways, and city. No sign of Catherine. He wanted to search for her himself, but politics stopped him from doing so.

Once he was king, nothing would stop him from finding her, even if he had to go all the way to England.

A knock sounded, and the door opened. His father walked in. "Are you ready?"

Malik took a deep breath. "As ready as I'll ever be."

"Son." His father touched his shoulder with a gentle hand. "I know these past few days have not been easy for you. Catherine is afraid of shaming you and our family. When she realizes there is no shame, she will be back."

"It's all right. I'll be fine." But would he? What if he couldn't find her? What if she refused to return with him? Doubts plagued his mind.

"No, you are not." His father grasped him by the shoulders. "Never underestimate what the right woman can do for you. Being crown prince isn't easy, and neither is being the king. Responsibility was heaped upon you from the day you were born. Your mother tried to keep you grounded, and she succeeded." Compassion filled his father's eyes. "I fear now your emotions are too controlled."

"A good king isn't controlled by his emotions, but by his intellect." That had been drummed into him enough over the years.

Jamal shook his head. "No, my son. Intellect is good, but emotions are what make us human, and what make the king a compassionate man. Over the years, your mother has been the one I can show my emotions to, as I know Catherine is for you. You will win her love."

"Yes, I will." Malik grasped his father's forearms. "But for today, I must be the crown prince. Tomorrow I will be king. Tomorrow I will find Catherine."

His father nodded with a smile on his face. Together they walked out of the suite and to the ballroom where the coronation party would take place.

Catherine smoothed her hands over the dress the dressmaker had sent over a couple of hours ago, as Samir waited. The beautiful white, gold, and red brought out the highlights in her hair and gave her confidence in herself as a beautiful woman. Three days was a long time to spend thinking, and away from Malik. How she thought she'd be able to live without him in her life, she'd never know.

She bit her lower lip and wondered for the thousandth time if showing up at the coronation party was such a good idea.

Yes, it was. Her spine stiffened. She'd finished giving an interview to the local paper hours ago, with assurances it would run in the morning edition.

"Everything is in place, Miss Taylor," Samir said.

Catherine glanced up. Samir looked very handsome in his dress uniform, which almost matched her clothing. The only difference was he had more red in his than gold.

Catherine smiled. Samir had been more than helpful over the last three days. He'd kept her secret, and in doing so, risked Malik's wrath. He, and he alone, knew of her plan. It was better this way, just in case it failed.

It wouldn't fail. She wouldn't allow it to. The herd of elephants in her stomach increased as Samir escorted her to the car. The ride to the palace was short. The next thing she knew they were outside the ballroom.

Music floated in the air; anticipation fought with excitement as well. The two guards at the door nodded as she passed. Catherine stopped just inside the room, taking in the crowd dressed to the nines for tonight's party.

Samir grasped her elbow.

"Thank you for the escort, Samir, but this is something I have to do alone."

"Of course." He bowed and stepped away.

Catherine took a deep breath as she took the first step. She heard a gasp, and then cameras clicked and flashes went off. She scanned the crowd and found Malik. It was now or never.

The room grew still, and then silence. Overwhelming silence pressed into him as the band stopped playing. Malik glanced up to see what was going on. Everyone was looking at the ballroom doors, and he turned his head in that direction.

His heart leapt in his chest.

Catherine! Was he dreaming?

She was bathed in artificial light from all the camera flashes constantly going off. He stared at her. Did she realize the significance of the outfit she wore? It was the traditional caftan the future crown princess would wear to meet her prince.

He couldn't tear his gaze from her, even as he started to walk toward her. He was conscious of her moving to him and the flashing of the cameras, but they didn't seem to bother her at all.

They met halfway. She stopped and then curtseyed.

He opened his mouth to speak, but she shook her head. Reaching over, she took his hand in hers. Her fingers trembled slightly as she placed his hand over her heart.

His own heart pounded as blood raced through his veins. Her hand covered his, against her chest. Malik held his breath. Did she realize what she was doing? The significance of this? In the silence all he could hear was his own labored breathing.

Fine tremors shook her body, and he wanted to pull her into his arms, but he couldn't. He needed to, no, *had* to, see this through to the end, because once it was finished, he was going to kiss her until she had no breath left.

"Crown Prince Malik al-Hakim." Her voice was clear and strong in the quiet room. "I, Catherine Taylor, accept your proposal of marriage."

A murmur went through the crowd as cameras continued to flash. Malik opened his mouth to speak, but she silenced him with a light kiss.

"I can't live without you, Malik. As long as I'm with you, nothing else matters. Not the press, not my past. Nothing. You are all that matters to me."

Malik found his voice. "By your public declaration. I acknowledge that you are my choice as wife and queen."

He took her free hand, placed it over his heart, and covered it with his own. He struggled to finish the words he needed to say to make it official. All he wanted to do was gather her up into his arms, kiss her, and then demand she never leave him again. "I, Malik al-Hakim," he said, the words flowing from his lips, "accept you as my bride and the love of my life."

A cheer went up from the crowd, and Malik gathered her into his arms. "You didn't have to do this," he whispered in her ear.

"Yes, I did." She leaned back and gazed at him. "I love you, Malik."

"You got that right." He spun her around in his arms. "I love you so much, and there is no backing out now. Within minutes the entire world will know you're my choice and my queen." Joy flowed through his veins, along with excitement and anticipation.

"I wouldn't want it any other way." She smiled with tears in her eyes.

Malik shook his head. He would never understand her, but then that should make life interesting. He lowered his lips to hers.

Cheers from those inside the ballroom and outside became louder. Malik tightened his arms around Catherine as the kiss went on. This was their time.

ACKNOWLEDGMENTS

As always to my critique group, Chandra, Isabel and Nia. You ladies are the best.

ABOUT THE AUTHOR

Marie Tuhart lives in the beautiful Pacific Northwest with her muse, Penny, a four-pound toy poodle. Marie loves to read and write. When she's not writing, she spends time with family, traveling and enjoying life.

Marie is a multi-published author with The Wild Rose Press, Trifecta Publishing House, and she does some self-publishing. To be alerted on new releases, you can join Marie's newsletter where she gives her group advance information on her books, runs contests, and does giveaways just for her newsletter readers. Marie can also be found on Goodreads, Pinterest, Twitter, and Facebook.

www.ingramcontent.com/pod-product-compliance
Lightning Source LLC
Chambersburg PA
CBHW050348190726
48284CB00007BB/2191